"Sweetheame."

The way his   he was
joking, but h   y at his
gentle teasir

They headed toward the first ride. The park wasn't as crowded as it would be later, but a few groups still stood in line in front of the brightly colored Ferris wheel.

"Why do they keep stopping with people at the top?"

"It's part of the fun," she told him, laughing when he gave her a look like she might be out of her mind. "Don't tell me you're afraid of heights..."

"Oh, I'm afraid of plenty," he answered. "Going back to Starlight. Losing my family's bank. Torpedoing my career with this extended vacation. The fallout from kissing you again."

She drew in a sharp breath, shocked by both his honesty and what he'd said about kissing her.

"You're trying to distract me."

"Or myself," he countered.

Suddenly the ride operator motioned them to load into the empty passenger car.

When Finn didn't move, Kaitlin took his hand and led him forward. "One step at a time."

WELCOME TO STARLIGHT:
They swore they'd never fall in love...
but promises were made to be broken!

Dear Reader,

Welcome to Starlight, Washington. It was such fun to dream up this cozy town nestled in the Cascade Mountains and I'm thrilled to invite you to spend some time here.

A decade ago, three friends made a pact never to fall in love. Each one's heart had been crushed and they committed to protecting themselves from any more hurt the only way they knew how. Ten years later, they are back together in their hometown, and for Finn Samuelson, Parker Johnson and Nick Dunlap, the bond they shared remains as strong as ever. The circumstances of their lives might be different, but reuniting in their hometown will force each of them to break down their defenses and open their hearts to love in ways they never expected.

Finn Samuelson doesn't plan to stay in Starlight long, but when his estranged father falls ill, Finn's sense of duty forces him to step in and help save the bank that's been his family's legacy for generations.

Standing in his way is Kaitlin Carmody, a stranger with a mysterious past who has somehow become his father's trusted ally. Finn wants to believe that Kaitlin is responsible for the troubles at the bank. Maybe blaming her will take the edge off the guilt plaguing him for staying away from Starlight for so long. Soon Kaitlin's feisty spirit breaks down Finn's walls and he must decide whether to risk his heart or remain cut off from love as he vowed ten years earlier.

I love to hear from readers. You can find me at www.michellemajor.com.

All the best,

Michelle

The Best Intentions

Michelle Major

HARLEQUIN

SPECIAL
EDITION

HARLEQUIN®
SPECIAL
EDITION™

PLEASE RECYCLE • THIS PRODUCT IS RECYCLABLE

Recycling programs
for this product may
not exist in your area.

ISBN-13: 978-1-335-89442-7

The Best Intentions

Copyright © 2020 by Michelle Major

This edition published by arrangement with Harlequin Books S.A.

For questions and comments about the quality of this book,
please contact us at CustomerService@Harlequin.com.

Harlequin Enterprises ULC
22 Adelaide St. West, 40th Floor
Toronto, Ontario M5H 4E3, Canada
www.Harlequin.com

Printed in U.S.A.

Michelle Major grew up in Ohio but dreamed of living in the mountains. Soon after graduating with a degree in journalism, she pointed her car west and settled in Colorado. Her life and house are filled with one great husband, two beautiful kids, a few furry pets and several well-behaved reptiles. She's grateful to have found her passion writing stories with happy endings. Michelle loves to hear from her readers at michellemajor.com.

Books by Michelle Major

Harlequin Special Edition

Maggie & Griffin

Falling for the Wrong Brother
Second Chance in Stonecreek
A Stonecreek Christmas Reunion

Crimson, Colorado

Anything for His Baby
A Baby and a Betrothal
Always the Best Man
Christmas on Crimson Mountain
Romancing the Wallflower
Sleigh Bells in Crimson
Coming Home to Crimson

The Fortunes of Texas: Rambling Rose

Fortune's Fresh Start

Visit the Author Profile page
at Harlequin.com for more titles.

To Lana. I couldn't do it without you.

Chapter One

"To Daniel's memory."

Finn Samuelson raised his beer bottle and clinked it against Parker Johnson's before throwing an expectant look toward Nick Dunlap.

Nick shook his head, the flames from the firepit in his backyard crackling in the silence.

It had been ten years since Finn had been together with his two best friends from high school in their hometown, a decade in which he hadn't once returned to Starlight, Washington. He hated that it had taken the death of another former classmate to finally lure him back, top on his long list of current regrets.

"Come on, Nick," Parker urged. "Daniel's gone, and despite what's come to light, no one deserves that. You can honor his memory and still be loyal to Brynn."

Finn watched Nick's knuckles tighten around his beer, but finally he lifted it in a half-hearted salute. "Whatever," he muttered. "I know too much to believe there was anything honorable about Daniel Hale at this point."

"Have you talked to Brynn?" Finn asked.

"Other than knocking on her door in the middle of the night to deliver the news that her husband lost control of his truck out at Devil's Landing leaving her a widow and single mother?" Nick gave a sharp shake of his head. "Uh, no. That was about the extent of it."

Finn had driven the switchback road through the nearby Cascade Mountains dozens of times in high school. He pictured the hairpin turn where Daniel had gone over and inwardly cringed. He didn't envy his friend, who was Starlight's police chief, having to make that kind of visit to anyone, let alone the woman who'd once been his best friend. "Do you think she knew about the affair?" Daniel had died in the crash, along with the truck's passenger, who'd turned out to be his mistress.

Nick sighed. "It wasn't his first. She might not

have known about this one, but she understood the type of guy she'd married."

"It's still hard to believe the two of you aren't friends anymore." Finn took a pull of his beer. "She was like your shadow back in high school."

"We're friends, but things change," Nick answered, his voice tight. "Neither of you has bothered to come back here in way too long."

"Everything feels the same to me," Parker muttered. "My dad has been gone for years, but as soon as I pull into town I start to sweat. I can still feel the force of his disapproval like he's waiting for me to come home so he can tell me what a screwup I am."

"Except you're not," Finn reminded him.

"Somehow that's hard to remember in Starlight."

Finn could relate to his friend's sentiment. No one from his life in Seattle would believe that Finn Samuelson, prominent investment banker about to make partner at his prestigious firm, was a huge disappointment to his own father. Finn's decision to leave his hometown instead of remaining heir apparent to the local bank his family had owned for decades had caused a seemingly irreparable rift in his already strained relationship with his dad.

He knew Parker's situation had been even worse. Although Jeff Johnson had been Starlight's mayor for several terms, Parker's dad had been cruel and abusive to his wife behind closed doors. Even after he'd died of a sudden heart attack their senior year, Parker had been as desperate to leave his childhood behind as Finn. In fact, Nick was the only one of the three to stay in Starlight.

Returning caused an itch under Finn's skin that he couldn't manage to scratch. Sure, a part of him missed the quiet and the beauty of the valley. Seattle was gorgeous, but between the crowded city and the frenetic pace of his job, Finn rarely found time to take a moment to appreciate it. Even the air in Starlight seemed fresher, pine-scented and tangy. Every breath brought memories of his childhood, both good and bad.

"Have you seen your dad?" Nick glanced at him over the rim of his bottle.

"I'd hoped he'd be at the funeral," Finn admitted, shaking his head. "Hoped and dreaded in equal measure, I guess. I figured if I talked to him there and he said something to set me off, I could leave again with a clear conscience."

Nick raised a thick brow. "No such luck?"

"He didn't show. Back in the day I remember him making the whole family go to every funeral of a bank customer. He told us it was part of his role in the community."

Parker let out a humorless laugh. "If I had a

nickel for all the times my dad force-marched us out to solidify his loving family-man mayor routine, I'd be rich."

"You're already rich," Finn reminded his friend.

"The divorce business has been good to me," Parker conceded. "I like making people happy."

"You're delusional." Nick laughed. "Divorce doesn't make people happy."

"It does if those people are miserable in their marriages."

"Speaking of…" Finn placed his empty beer bottle on the patio, leaning back in the Adirondack chair where he sat. Nick had bought this house from his grandparents a few years ago and it backed up to one of the local fishing lakes. Water lapped rhythmically against the rocky shoreline at the bottom of the hill.

"Don't tell us you're getting married," Nick interrupted.

Finn laughed when both his friends shot him equally horrified glances. "No," he assured them. "Although it's expected at the firm. Marry a socially appropriate wife, have a couple of adorable kids and join the country club."

Nick made a gagging sound in the back of his throat. "That sounds like the life my parents wanted for me. I still think they believe law enforcement is a passing fancy."

"You just need to explain that you've got a thing for handcuffs," Finn said, earning a one-finger salute from Nick. "Marriage might not be your choice but once I make partner, it's part of the deal. Which is why I want to talk about the pact."

Parker let out a low whistle and picked up the bottle of whiskey that sat next to his chair. "I need something stronger than craft beer for this conversation."

"It's not complicated," Finn said as his friend poured the liquor and passed a shot glass to each of them. "Have you fallen in love?"

"Of course not," Parker scoffed.

"You?" Finn transferred his gaze to Nick.

"We know Tricky Nicky hasn't given away his heart," Parker answered before Nick had a chance to speak. "He's still hung up on Brynn."

"I'm not hung up on her," Nick said through gritted teeth. "We never even dated."

"Yeah," Parker agreed, running a hand through his blond hair. "Thanks to the fact that you set her up with Daniel. If you hadn't been too busy working your way through the cheerleading squad—"

"That's not what I was doing." Nick pushed out of the chair, fists clenched tight as he took a step around the firepit toward Parker. "Brynn and I were friends. Nothing more, then or now."

Parker looked like he wanted to argue but Finn reached out and swatted his arm. "Give it a rest.

She buried her husband today. Nothing's going to change right now."

"Or ever," Nick added, a razor-sharp edge to his voice.

"Fine," Parker agreed after a moment. "Sorry for bringing up a sensitive subject. I've been in the courtroom too long. It's second nature to push people's buttons."

"Apology accepted." Nick flexed his hands, then crossed his arms over his chest. "Just leave my buttons alone." He turned toward Finn. "I haven't fallen in love or even come close, although I think that has less to do with our pact and more to do with the fact that I'm happy not being tied down to one woman."

Parker leaned forward in his chair. "I spend most of my life seeing the worst about falling in love. There's no way in hell I'm getting tangled up like that."

"But the pact doesn't rule out marriage, right?" Finn asked quietly.

"You're a grown man," Nick pointed out. "Some stupid, drunken promise we made after high school shouldn't stop you from falling in love if that's what floats your boat."

"I'm not talking about love," Finn clarified. "I'm expected to get married. While it would be great if the woman I choose is a decent human being, I'm not planning on going all romance hero at this point."

"I like it," Parker said with a nod. "Very eighteenth century of you. It's like a business contract. That could actually work a hell of a lot better than leading with your heart."

"Exactly." Finn waited for relief to fill him that someone else understood his plan. It had been a night much like this one when the three of them had made their pact. After making the rounds of graduation parties, they'd gone out to one of the Forest Service campgrounds with a bottle of cheap whiskey. They'd survived high school, but not without their individual scars.

Finn had just revealed to his father that he wanted no part of the family business. His dad had reacted with angry threats and a convincing promise that Finn's mom would have been sorely disappointed in her only son if she'd lived to see him break his father's heart. Finn's own chest had ached at the knowledge that his father wanted nothing to do with him if he wasn't contributing to the bank's bottom line.

As committed to leaving Starlight as Finn, Parker had been struggling with guilt over the death of his dad. Guilt because a big part of him was relieved to finally have his family free of the emotional abuse they'd endured for years. But

Finn knew his friend also harbored a secret fear that he'd inherited not only his late father's eye color but also his temper and the darkness that had seeped from his soul. Finn didn't believe it for a minute, but Parker wouldn't be convinced otherwise.

Nick's heartbreak had been the most straightforward. He'd pushed the girl who'd had a crush on him for years into the arms of another guy, only to realize the depth of his feelings for her once she was gone. But Brynn was pregnant and she and Daniel had just announced their engagement, cutting off any future Nick might have had with her.

They'd been a pathetic trio, committed to never suffering from disappointment, rejection or heartbreak again. Parker had been the one to suggest the pact against falling in love. He was convinced that if they eliminated that sort of deep emotion, they'd stay safe from future pain.

At the time, it had seemed like a joke to Finn, but he'd played along. Through the years, the drunken promise had become an excuse he'd used whenever a girlfriend got too close or wanted more than he was willing to give. No falling in love. Easy enough, and if he kept that oath clear in his mind, maybe he could do what was expected by his boss and still keep his heart out of the mix.

"I wouldn't bother with marriage in the first place," Nick announced into the silence. "But at least you've got Parker's number when things don't work out."

"You never know how things are going to work out," Finn answered, dread pooling in his gut at the thought of facing his father.

Even in the dim light cast by the fire, he could see the pain that shadowed Nick's gaze.

"To the unknown," Parker said, raising his glass.

Finn lifted his in response, then downed the amber liquid, hissing softly as the whiskey burned his throat. "To the unknown."

Kaitlin Carmody reached for her coffee mug, sighing when she found it empty. She had a strict personal rule about limiting her caffeine intake to one cup a day, although she could use another jolt of energy. She'd already been at her desk three hours, and it wasn't even ten in the morning.

Her ex-boyfriend would have snickered at her attempt at restraint. When she and Robbie had been together, *excess* had been the word best used to describe their bond. Alcohol, drugs, sex… Often all three at the same time. That had been rock bottom, and Kaitlin was proud of how far she'd come. How much she'd abandoned—basically everything—to start over in Starlight.

Two years ago, she'd been working as a barista in one of Seattle's ubiquitous coffee shops when a customer had left behind a Washington State map. While refolding the slick paper, her gaze had snagged on a dot east of the city, the name Starlight printed next to it.

Something tiny and almost unrecognizable had begun to unfurl inside her as she traced her fingers over the shiny letters. Kaitlin didn't have much experience with hope, but she recognized it just the same. That night, she'd loaded her meager belongings into a backpack and the next morning set off out of the city and toward her new beginning, leaving a note for Robbie not to look for her.

"Earth to the woman in the gray dress."

She glanced up as the deep voice invaded her meandering thoughts. Her breath caught in her throat at the sight of the imposing man frowning down at her. Dark hair, piercing blue eyes and broad shoulders that looked almost out of place contained in the expensive suit he wore.

"Sorry," she said automatically, then inwardly cringed. Jack had told her she needed to stop saying sorry for everything, that it showed a weakness and self-doubt she shouldn't let people see. But apologies still rolled off her tongue like a snowball down an alpine ski slope. "I was daydreaming," she continued with a half smile, as if that wasn't totally obvious. As if she owed this tense stranger an explanation.

"Right," he agreed. "You get what you pay for."

Ouch. So much for the pleasantries of casual conversation. Kaitlin straightened her shoulders. "Can I help you?"

"Is he in?" The man inclined his head toward Jack's office.

"Do you have an appointment?"

One side of the stranger's full mouth curved up. "Not exactly."

"Mr. Samuelson has a busy calendar," she lied. Despite her resolve to be different than she used to be, lying still came naturally to Kaitlin. A fact that had worked in her favor the past six months. "If you leave your name and number, I can get you added to his schedule."

"He'll see me now," the man insisted, his gaze locked on the closed oak door.

Kaitlin might be good at apologies, but she was even better at standing her ground when the situation called for it. This situation called for it.

"I don't think that's a good idea." She stood, moving quickly to block the man's progress.

He blinked, as if he'd never had anyone deny him a request before. She could well imagine that no woman had ever denied him.

One smoldering glance from those blue eyes

framed by heavy brows and model-sharp cheek-bones and most of the women she knew would melt in a puddle at his feet.

Good thing Kaitlin wasn't much of a melter any longer.

"Are you going to step aside?" he asked, one dark brow arching. "Or shall I move you?"

"I'm going with door number three," she told him with her phoniest smile. "Leave your name and number. I'll put you on Mr. Samuelson's sched-ule." Out of the corner of her eye she could see that one of the personal bankers, Missy, had come out of her office and was waving at Kaitlin as if to warn her of something.

Kaitlin didn't melt and she refused to back down. Not after everything Jack Samuelson had done for her. No one in the office might understand why the bank's owner needed her protection, but it didn't change the fact that he did.

The stranger took a step toward her. "I'm see-ing him now."

She narrowed her eyes. "You lay a hand on me, and I'll call the police so fast it will make your smug head spin."

"I have Nick Dunlap's cell number," he said evenly. "Would you like me to dial?"

Why would this guy know Starlight's police chief so well? She studied him for a moment longer, then stifled a gasp. Those bright blue eyes and thick brows… She knew another man who had them.

"Who are you?" she whispered.

"Finn Samuelson," he answered. "And if you'll excuse me, I'm going to see my dad."

Jack's estranged son was back. Heart hammering in her chest, Kaitlin automatically took a step away and watched Jack's estranged son walk past her and enter his father's office. The door closed behind him with a decisive click.

Chapter Two

Finn drew a shallow breath as he stepped into his father's inner sanctum. The office still smelled of polished wood and judgment, as if the cherry bookshelves and executive desk held him up for appraisal, only to find him lacking.

He gave a small shake of his head, the thought that the bank held any sway over him after so many years preposterous. He sniffed again and caught the faint scent of vanilla, like the woman who was his father's gatekeeper had tried to infuse the space with a bit of warmth.

Good luck with that.

His father hadn't turned around in the oversize leather chair that sat behind the desk. Finn glanced out at the view of downtown Starlight. The main lobby of the bank operated on the ground level, with executive offices and private banking handled from the second floor.

Finn had worked summers and holidays in the bank all through high school, but he'd avoided his dad's office. There were too many reminders of the past and the legacy he never believed was his due. Photos of his relatives lined the bookshelves, including several of his great-great-grandparents at the bank's grand opening. Starlight had been little more than a pit stop for pioneers back then. First Trust had seen the town through booms and busts and remained an institution he'd always link with his past.

He cleared his throat, but his father still didn't turn. Had the far-too-pretty assistant somehow warned him about Finn's arrival? She seemed pit bull protective, but he couldn't imagine her as a master of mental telepathy. Unfortunately, he easily imagined her as the master of every one of his fantasies.

He couldn't pinpoint what it was about the beautiful blonde with the milk-chocolate eyes and curves for miles, but his immediate awareness of her had gone way beyond sensible. If she was on Team Jack Samuelson, clearly Finn needed to keep his distance.

"Hey, Dad," he said, frowning when he got no response.

He stepped around the desk and his heart froze. His father's head was bent forward, eyes closed and hands in prayer position over his chest. His hair was almost pure white, deep lines fanning from his eyes. Somehow he'd aged a lifetime in the decade Finn had been gone.

There was no way...

"Dad!"

Finn sucked in a breath as his father startled at hearing his name shouted. He blinked several times, then glanced up at Finn. For a moment it was as if he didn't recognize his own son. Yes, it had been over ten years, but Finn had always resembled his dad's side of the family. Plus, this was his dad. What the hell...

"Finneas?" the older man whispered after a moment.

"Yeah." Finn concentrated on keeping his voice steady. "I'm in town for Daniel's funeral so I thought—"

Suddenly his father stood and wrapped his arms around Finn's shoulders. "Son. I've missed you."

"Um…okay." Finn swallowed back the ball of emotion welling in his throat. This certainly wasn't the reception he'd expected. He couldn't remember ever being hugged by his dad. A hearty clap on the shoulders was the most he'd gotten and that was after being named valedictorian of his senior class.

"Are you returning to Starlight?"

Now it was Finn's turn to blink. "No, Dad. My life is in Seattle. You know that." The delivery might be softer than before, but his father could still land an emotional punch like a prizefighter.

Jack stared at him for a moment, his eyes clear and far too familiar, searching for something Finn didn't know how to offer. Then he nodded and let out a long breath. "You always had bigger dreams than Starlight could make come true."

Finn gave a startled laugh. That was one of the nicest things his dad had ever said to him. Back in high school, Jack had seemed to take great pleasure in making Finn feel like there was something wrong with him for wanting more.

He stepped back, putting the desk between himself and his father. He needed some kind of a buffer. He'd imagined talking to his dad a million times since leaving Starlight. Never would he have guessed he'd feel anything but anger and bitterness. Where had this version of his father been when Finn needed him most?

"You're a big success in Seattle," Jack said, lowering himself back into the chair.

It was a statement, not a question, and the pride in his father's voice shocked Finn to the core.

"I'm on target to be named partner this year."

"Congratulations. We should have dinner tonight as an early celebration. Will you come to the house?"

"Sure," Finn answered, still dumbfounded. "I didn't think you'd—"

"Jack?"

Finn turned as his father's assistant entered the office. She darted a worried glance between the two of them, and he wondered how much she knew about his relationship with his dad.

"Kaitlin, have you met my son?" His father leaned forward in his chair. "He's a big-shot banker in Seattle."

"You've mentioned that," she said, walking forward. She shoved her hand toward Finn, her gaze trained on the middle of his chest instead of looking him in the eye. He was oddly disappointed. "I'm Kaitlin Carmody. I work for your dad. Obviously."

"Finn Samuelson," he replied, trying not to notice the softness of her skin as he shook her hand. "You're not from Starlight."

"No," she confirmed, snatching back her hand. He couldn't figure out why she seemed so nervous.

"Jack, you have an appointment with Ernie in the mayor's office."

"Right," his father agreed. "I guess Finn isn't the only big shot around here. The bank is underwriting the Starlight Art Festival."

Finn frowned at the comparison, then noticed Kaitlin's mouth thin. "You haven't committed to anything yet," she told Jack. "You wanted to ensure they were going to have appropriate marketing and signage."

He waved a hand as he stood. "I don't need reminding," he snapped. "This is my bank and I can still make the best decisions for its future."

There was the Jack Samuelson that Finn remembered.

"Of course," Kaitlin said softly.

"I could show you a thing or two about the art of a deal." Jack pointed to Finn, then straightened his tie. "We'll compare notes over dinner. Kaitlin will have the food ready at seven. Don't be late."

Without another word for either of them, Finn's dad left the office, his gait slow and measured.

"You cook for him?" Finn asked, his mind reeling.

"Um…" Color flooded Kaitlin's cheeks. "Sometimes."

What was he missing about this woman's relationship with his dad? He couldn't put a finger on it, but some instinct made him certain there was more to it than she was admitting. "But you're his assistant at the bank," he prompted.

She nodded.

"Are you his girlfriend, too?" he forced himself to ask.

Her mouth dropped open before she snapped it shut. "Of course not. He's old enough to be my dad."

He didn't bother to point out that plenty of women dated older men. The second wife of AmeriNat's North American CEO, a man in his early sixties, was younger than Finn.

"How long have you been at the bank?"

She crossed her arms over her chest. "Two years," she mumbled.

"Your background is in finance?"

She started to shake her head, then stopped, her shoulders going stiff. "Is there a reason for this interrogation?"

Finn ran a hand through his hair. "I haven't seen my dad for over ten years, but he's different than he used to be. I'm trying to figure out why."

"I don't know what you're talking about," she muttered. "Jack is exactly the same as he's always been."

"Then you don't know Jack," he whispered.

She huffed out a small laugh at his pitiful joke, and the sound reverberated through him. He didn't want to have that kind of visceral response to Kaitlin Carmody but couldn't seem to stop himself.

"I need to get back to work," she said with a pointed look.

"Sure," he agreed, thoughts and emotions pinging through his mind. The physical changes were to be expected, but it was the transformation of his father's personality that shocked him. Maybe the change in his dad had nothing to do with Kaitlin, but Finn remained unconvinced.

With a last look around the office, he slowly walked out, aware that Kaitlin followed like she was herding a recalcitrant child.

"I'll see you tonight," he said, studying her classically beautiful features for a hint of…something. She flashed a tight grin and her dark eyes gave nothing away.

"Tonight," she agreed.

Feeling summarily dismissed, he started down the hall, stopping to chat with several people who had worked at the bank for as long as he could remember.

The atmosphere was so different than his Seattle office. He got hugs and a few cheek pinches, made congratulatory remarks about graduations, weddings and grandchildren. Despite his absence, people treated him like he'd only been away for a short time instead of a decade.

In Seattle, his coworkers kept to themselves. Finn was management and had been pegged as the future of the division. That put a wall between him and everyone below him on the company totem pole, and until this moment he hadn't realized how much it bothered him.

He might not have wanted the First Trust of Starlight as his future, but could appreciate the warm and welcoming atmosphere he associated with everyone except his dad. Now he was starting to doubt his own memories. Maybe his father hadn't been as bad as he'd once thought. Jack might not have made updating the decor a priority, but he certainly engendered loyalty from his staff.

Was it possible the problem had actually been with Finn the whole time? As he walked out into the bright morning sunshine, he shook off the thought. He needed to call his sister. The last he'd heard from her, Ella was working at a hospital in a speck of a town somewhere in Argentina. She hadn't put down roots since leaving Starlight, constantly traveling and spending months in remote parts of the world.

They managed to keep in touch whenever she

had internet or cell service but could go long stretches without any type of communication. That didn't change the bond they shared, and Ella would gladly remind him of all of their father's faults.

He glanced up and down Starlight's main street. There was a stoplight on the north end of downtown that hadn't been there when he'd left. The mountains loomed in the distance as the light turned from red to green. Otherwise, the town looked much the same as he remembered. Some of the businesses had changed, but otherwise he felt as though he'd stepped back into a scene from his youth.

A gang of kids on mountain bikes rode by, happy voices and laughter trailing on the air in their wake. It reminded him of so many summer days when he, Parker and Nick had ridden for miles, exploring the trails and back roads surrounding the town.

Would his hypothetical children have that kind of freedom? Most of his coworkers' kids seemed overscheduled and often glued to their devices, a sad shell of a childhood in Finn's opinion.

He massaged a hand along the back of his neck. He was getting ahead of himself. He didn't even have a wife, let alone kids. This trip to his hometown was supposed to clear out his emotional roadblocks so he could move ahead on both fronts. Right on schedule.

It was funny, actually. He'd bristled against his dad's expectations and what he considered the proverbial prison of First Trust, but he was chained to his job in a way that would have horrified his younger self.

As he headed toward his BMW sedan, he told himself he'd chosen his life, which made all the difference. Too bad he was having trouble believing that at the moment.

"You're Finn Samuelson, right?"

Finn turned as a middle-aged man approached from the entrance of the bank.

"That's right."

"Doug Meyer," the man said, holding out a hand. "I'm your dad's vice president."

"Nice to meet you," Finn said with a practiced smile. Doug had the job that would have been Finn's at this point if he hadn't left. He had no right to be annoyed, but he was anyway.

"I was wondering if I could bend your ear for a few minutes about a situation at the bank?"

Finn grimaced. "You must know I have no involvement at First Trust."

"Of course," Doug agreed quickly. "But it involves

your father. I'm concerned about his recent behavior. Some things have changed."

Like Jack Samuelson had grown a heart?

"Your dad won't discuss the issues, and Kaitlin goes into dragon mode whenever I approach, so—"

"What does Kaitlin have to do with this?" Finn asked, his gut tightening.

"I'm not exactly certain, but things aren't good. Someone has to do something. Maybe you can help."

Hell, no.

Finn should walk away right now. He wanted nothing to do with the bank or any suspected problems in his father's life, especially not if they had to do with Kaitlin Carmody.

"I have some time," he answered, unable to stop himself.

Doug nodded. "Let's grab a cup of coffee." He pointed down the street toward the sign that said Main Street Perk. "I'd rather not get tongues wagging at the office."

"Fine." Finn fell in step with the shorter man, willing away the tension that crowded his shoulders. Whatever Doug had to say, Finn would listen, then politely explain he didn't want to be involved. No problem.

* * *

Kaitlin dragged in a shuddery breath as the doorbell at Jack's sprawling ranch-style house rang later that night.

She glanced out the kitchen window to where her boss practiced his putt on the tightly mowed green he'd had installed last year. Okay, she was answering the door.

Easy enough.

She dried her hands on a nearby dish towel and headed through the kitchen and down the hall toward the foyer. She should have known Finn immediately. Jack didn't have many photos on display, but there were enough of a young Finn, his sister, Ella, and Jack's late wife, Katie, to recognize the man the boy had grown into.

She'd been caught off guard. That never would have happened before life in Starlight turned her soft and trusting. Bouncing in and out of foster care as a kid, Kaitlin had learned always to be on the alert for threats.

Although it made no sense, every instinct for danger she had gave off warning lights when she thought about Finn.

Plastering on a bright smile, she opened the door.

For a moment, he appeared nonplussed before

his features tightened into a flat mask. "Playing lady of the manor?" he asked with that irritating brow lift.

She let her smile fade. If Jack's son didn't want to play nice, why should she? "Don't look shocked. He told you I was helping with dinner."

"I just wonder what else you're helping with," he said as he followed her through the house. "Or maybe 'helping yourself to' is more accurate."

She spun on her heel so fast he practically plowed into her. This close, she could see the gray flecks in his blue eyes and feel the heat coming off him. He'd changed into a polo shirt and faded jeans, but the casual dress did nothing to make him less intimidating.

Kaitlin hated being intimidated.

"What does that mean?" she demanded.

"I think you know."

"You're wrong." Wrong on so many levels, she wanted to add. Her track record with morals and good judgment was spotty at best, but she'd changed since coming to Starlight. Jack had given her a chance, and she'd never take advantage of that, no matter what vague insinuations his son made.

"What the hell's going on here?"

She turned at the sound of Jack's booming voice.

"Your *assistant* and I are getting to know each other," Finn answered, and she heard a thread of temper lacing his tone.

She glanced over her shoulder. "Tell me you didn't use air quotes."

He shot her a quelling glare. "Do I look like I need hand gestures to convey my distaste?"

"You look like you need a swift kick in the back end," Jack called. "Both of you get in the kitchen."

"There's the dad I remember," Finn said under his breath as he stalked after her.

"You obviously bring out the best in him," she shot back, then pressed her lips together. Why was she engaging in this verbal sparring with Finn? She'd have better luck waving a stick at an angry mountain lion.

"I asked Kaitlin to make your mother's shepherd's pie recipe," Jack announced as they entered the kitchen. "We'll eat and then talk."

"I'm not really hungry," Finn muttered.

"You were always hungry," Jack countered. "It's been a lot of years since you've been in the house, but I can't imagine that's changed."

She heard something that sounded like a stomach growling, and Jack let out a satisfied chuckle. "There's a bottle of wine on the dining room table," he told Finn. "You open it while Kaitlin finishes with the food. I'll be right back."

She glanced toward Jack, but he waved off her obvious concern. "I'm fine. Just need to check something in my office."

Kaitlin grabbed two pot holders from the counter and moved toward the stove. Maybe she should have refused to make a dish that had been one of Finn's mother's signatures. Honestly, she hadn't thought about Finn's reaction. She simply liked cooking in the homey kitchen and using the recipes that Katie Samuelson had written on index cards in her precise cursive.

Carrying the casserole into the dining room, she purposely avoided eye contact with Finn. She set the dish on the trivet she'd placed on the table and turned back toward the kitchen to retrieve the side dishes.

"There are three places set," Finn announced from the head of the table, his voice a low growl.

"Jack invited me to stay for dinner."

"You called him Mr. Samuelson at the bank earlier today."

"What's your point?" Finn's attitude caused every one of her hackles to rise.

"Leave the girl alone," Jack said as he entered the dining room from the far door.

Finn popped the cork on the wine. "I think it's time she left you alone."

Kaitlin felt a blush stain her cheeks. She knew

there were questions about the nature of her relationship with Jack but mainly ignored the gossip. It bothered her that Finn had so quickly heard the rumors, even if most of what was said wasn't true.

"You have no idea what you're talking about," Jack said with a shake of his head.

"Why don't you fill me in?"

As Finn poured the wine, Kaitlin met Jack's gaze across the table. For a moment he let down his guard, and she saw both fear and frustration in his tired eyes. She gave him a small smile and nodded, as if her opinion of how he should handle this conversation would matter.

His mouth thinned as he looked away, and she sighed. If Jack didn't tell Finn the whole truth of his situation, it would only cause more trouble for all of them.

She moved to the kitchen and picked up the salad bowl and basket of bread still sitting on the counter. When she returned, both Jack and Finn stood next to their chairs, clearly waiting for her to sit first. The reminder that both of these men were gentlemen despite the tension between them was like a slap in the face.

Kaitlin didn't belong here, even if Jack wanted her to. "I'm going to the guesthouse," she announced.

"We haven't even started dinner," Jack told her.

"You need to eat after all the time it took to make the food."

"Wait." Finn held up a hand. "You live here?"

"Don't go there," she warned.

"I'll go wherever I want," he shot back.

Kaitlin opened her mouth to deliver a snappy retort, but Jack's howling laughter stopped her. Finn seemed just as surprised at the sound, and they both turned to the older man.

"I remember all the times you and Ella squabbled over the dinner table," he said, swiping a hand across his cheek. "It used to annoy me to no end. I'd get home after a long day at the bank, and there was no peace and quiet to be found."

"Kaitlin isn't my sister," Finn ground out.

No doubt, Kaitlin thought to herself. As much of a pompous jerk as she found Finn to be, her awareness of him was anything but brotherly.

"I still can't believe I miss the arguing," Jack said, more to himself than either of them. "Kaitlin, sit down. Let's have a civil dinner."

Jack had given her a chance to make a new life in Starlight, and she owed him her loyalty but also knew he was using her as a buffer. "Not tonight," she told him gently. "You two have some catching up to do. I'll only get in the way."

"Amen," Finn said at the same time Jack answered, "You won't."

"I'll see you in the morning," she told her boss, doing her best to ignore the weight of Finn's stare. Jack looked like he wanted to argue but finally nodded, and Kaitlin walked away, hoping the two men could manage to get through the meal without killing each other.

Chapter Three

The knock came at close to midnight, according to the clock on her nightstand.

Kaitlin struggled to wake, then shot up in bed, her first thought that something had happened to Jack.

The guesthouse was more of a tiny apartment, with a cozy living area on one side and a small bedroom situated off the kitchen. She stumbled to the floor, the sheet still wrapped around her legs.

"I'm coming," she shouted, flipping on a light before hurrying across the wide-plank floor and— ouch—stubbing her toe on an uneven strip of oak.

When she wrenched open the door, Finn stood on the other side, tall and brooding and staring at her like she'd just made her escape from some kind of circus sideshow.

"Is your dad okay?" she whispered, worry clawing at her chest. She and Jack had been through some rough nights together, and although she knew he was healthy now, those times were difficult not to revisit.

"My guess is he's sleeping," Finn told her with a scowl. "Sorry I woke you."

She took a deep breath to calm herself and studied him, standing on the porch with only moonlight to reveal his handsome features. She'd been sleeping fitfully, unwelcome visions of the man standing at her door causing her to toss and turn. "I doubt that," she murmured. "People don't normally knock on someone's door in the middle of the night without the intent to wake them."

"True," he agreed with a little half smile that suddenly reminded her she was standing in front of him in pajama shorts and a loose tank top with no bra.

As if reading her mind, his gaze trailed down the front of her, then quickly back to her face. A faint hint of pink tinged his cheeks. Was Finn Samuelson blushing? A strangled giggle escaped her lips at the thought.

"Can I come in?" he asked, a husky note to his voice that had goose bumps erupting along her skin.

Oh, yes, her body squealed.

"Nope," she breathed.

"Kaitlin."

Her name whispered in that deep tone made her feel far too hot and bothered even though the temperature had cooled off considerably from earlier in the day.

"Finn, why are you here?" She kept her arms at her sides, tamping down every feminine desire she had. She was no longer held captive by her impulses. Those had led to nothing for her but circling the drain.

"I couldn't sleep."

"They have pills and late-night movies for that."

"My dad has cancer."

Right. She sucked in a breath, his quiet words slamming into her with the force of a sledgehammer, and then took a step back so he could enter the small space.

"Tea or liquor?" she asked, gesturing for him to have a seat on the overstuffed sofa.

"Your choice."

She moved to the kitchen, plucking the teakettle from where it sat on the stove top and then filling it with water. After turning on the burner, she took her terry-cloth robe from the bathroom door and slipped into it. She couldn't figure out how to subtly put on a bra, so adding the shapeless layer over her tank top was the best she could do.

The noise from her movements seemed to echo in the quiet. A glance at Finn showed that he was staring in front of him, as if some invisible movie played that captured every bit of his attention.

She unwrapped two tea bags while waiting for the kettle to boil, then poured the steaming water into the mugs. She'd developed a taste for herbal tea since limiting caffeine, and there was no doubt this was a much safer choice than alcohol. The last thing she needed was her defenses softening when it came to this conversation and the man invading her tiny home.

"Cream or sugar?" she asked as she set the tray on the coffee table in front of Finn, like she was some kind of British duchess serving high tea at midnight to one of her upper-crust friends.

"No, thanks."

"So…" she began, lowering herself onto the cushion next to Finn and curling her legs under her. She made sure to keep as much distance as possible between them but imagined she could still feel the warmth coming off his body. He'd make a darn good personal space heater on a cold winter night.

"He said you're the only one who knows." Finn took a small sip of the tea, then muttered a curse.

"It's hot," she belatedly warned.

Up went that eyebrow again. "Trying to burn my tongue to shut me up?"

"No, actually," she said with a soft laugh. "I don't enjoy being the keeper of your father's secret."

"Why did he trust you with it and what made you agree?"

Kaitlin reached for her mug, wrapping her fingers around the warmth of the porcelain. "I came to Starlight on a whim with no idea of what the future held. Your dad and I met in a coffee shop. I was reading an old copy of *On the Road*, looking for inspiration, I guess."

"He lived his entire life in this town, but that was always his favorite book."

"Didn't do much for me," Kaitlin admitted, "and Jack and I had a lively discussion about my error in opinion."

That comment earned a real smile from Finn, transforming his face from brooding to boyish in an instant. "I can imagine."

She nodded. "I'm sure you can. He asked some questions and when I told him I'd come to Starlight to start over, he offered me a job as his assistant. Mary had retired a few weeks earlier."

"That woman terrified me most of my childhood," Finn said. "She and my dad were a great match."

"I've done okay filling her shoes," Kaitlin said. Then she amended, "Or at least I've tried. I noticed Jack getting tired more easily about a year after I started, and he was having some hip and chest pain that the doctor chalked up to old age, but obviously it was way more than that."

"Stage-three melanoma," Finn murmured.

"The doctors in Seattle gave him a few months, so I found an oncologist in San Francisco who was conducting a human trial called tumor targeting. I'm sure he told you he's officially in remission. But he missed a lot of time at the bank, traveling for treatment."

"You've gone with him on every trip?"

She nodded. "Without the chance your father gave me, I'm not sure where I'd be right now. I owe him a lot."

"What do you get for your loyalty?"

She tightened her grip on the mug. "I don't understand what you mean."

"What's in it for you? Are you hoping to be the next Mrs. Jack Samuelson?"

"No offense to your dad," she said through clenched teeth, "but gross."

"Think he'll change his will?"

She shook her head, strangely disappointed that he continued to think the worst of her. "It isn't like that, Finn. Why do you need to make me the bad guy in all this?"

He stared at her for several long seconds, flummoxed by the question. He hadn't actually come here tonight to accuse her of anything. After his father's big revelation, Finn had been numb.

He'd returned to Nick's house, where he was staying, but hadn't shared with his friend what he'd learned about his dad. He needed more time to process things, or so he told himself.

Parker had already gone back to Seattle, and Finn had planned to drive back tomorrow morning. But between the information Doug at the bank had shared and the news about his father, he didn't see how he could leave just yet.

"Why doesn't he seem to understand that the bank is failing?" he asked instead of answering the question.

She shrugged. "He knows but believes he can fix it. Your father has quite the streak of optimism after the cancer treatments worked so well."

"Doug believes the problems started after you came on board," Finn said, studying her.

She snorted, and the indelicate sound was strangely appealing. "He thinks I'm smart enough to take down a hundred-year-old banking institution? That's actually a compliment."

"Your past isn't exactly spotless."

Color stained her cheeks as she narrowed her eyes at him. "You researched me?"

"I had Nick plug in your name to a few law enforcement databases this afternoon."

"I wasn't a saint, but nothing in my past should make you believe I could manage what you're insinuating."

She said the words calmly, and he liked that she didn't make excuses for her mistakes. She was right, too. She'd been in and out of foster care, had a misdemeanor for vandalism on her record, but nothing serious.

"Maybe you should take a closer look at ol' Dougie-boy." She made a face. "That guy's a weasel in a bad suit."

Finn chuckled. Doug definitely wasn't a paragon of fashion, and Finn hadn't particularly liked him after hearing everything he had to say.

"My dad trusts you," he told her, "obviously with his life. I don't want to feel guilty for not having been here with him through the treatments, but what's happening at First Trust is more complicated than fraud. At this point, the depositors are at risk. I need to figure out what the hell is going on and make it right."

"It would be simple if you could place the blame on me," she answered, lifting the ceramic mug to her lips.

He should not be focusing on her lips. Or her sleep-tousled hair. Or the way the robe she'd put on kept gaping at the center to reveal the lacy edge of her thin tank top.

"True," he managed, shifting on the sofa and commanding his body to behave.

"Life is rarely simple."

"Also true."

She leaned forward to place her mug back on the coffee table, giving him a tantalizing glimpse of the swell of her breast. He needed to get back to Nick's and take a cold shower or maybe a dip in the mountain-runoff-fed lake behind the house.

"Why is it your responsibility to make this right?" she asked, worrying the sash of the robe between two fingers. "You haven't spoken to Jack in years."

"He's my dad," Finn said, still not quite able to believe the depth of his emotion around his father's illness.

"He loves you and your sister," Kaitlin said gently. "We talked a lot on the flights back and forth to San Francisco. He has so many regrets about how he behaved after your mother died."

"Regrets are a family tradition for the Samuelsons." Finn rubbed a hand over his eyes. "I'm hoping to let go of some of mine if I fix this."

"Does Jack want your help?"

"What do you think?"

"He's proud, and cancer has taken a lot out of him."

"Yeah." Finn sighed. "But I have to do it."

She didn't say anything, but the quiet way she watched him, her brown eyes gentle, made his heart hammer in his chest.

"I want you to help me," he blurted.

"You don't trust me," she said with a laugh.

"My dad does, and that's a start."

She looked down, and a stray lock of hair fell forward to brush her cheek. He couldn't help himself. He reached out and tucked the soft strands behind her ear. His fingers grazed her cheek and it was all he could do to resist leaning in to claim her mouth with his.

Earlier today this woman seemed like a threat to his father and the bank. Now it felt like she was the only true ally Finn could rely on. How the hell had that happened, and was it his libido leading?

He snatched back his hand and stood.

"We don't have to be friends," he said, more for himself than her. "But if you truly care about my father, you'll help me figure out what's going on at the bank. It would kill him to lose it."

She stood, pulling the robe tight over her chest. "Okay," she whispered, and the breathless note to her voice sent all of Finn's blood south.

"Then I'll see you tomorrow."

"Tomorrow," she repeated, tugging her lower lip between her teeth.

Finn swallowed a groan. "Good night, Kaitlin," he said in a rush of breath.

Before she could answer or he could do something stupid like drag her into his arms, he turned and walked out into the night.

Chapter Four

"I put in an extra shot because you look like you're coming off a long night."

Kaitlin smiled gratefully as she took the paper cup from her friend Mara Reed, who also happened to be the best barista at Main Street Perk, Starlight's local coffee shop.

She didn't bother to mention that the extra caffeine would negate her one-cup limit. Kaitlin had suffered enough hard knocks that she knew the value of appreciating an unexpected kindness.

This whole town was filled with kindness and generosity, at least compared to the life she'd left behind in Seattle. She thanked Mara, then looked away when tears sprang to her eyes.

How embarrassing. She needed to pull herself together. She'd dealt with far worse than the mistrust she saw in Finn Samuelson's movie-star-handsome gaze. Why was having her motives and morals called into question affecting her so strongly?

"Hey, Jana," Mara called to the teenager filling the napkin dispenser next to the coffee bar. "I need five minutes. Can you cover the register?"

"Sure," the girl said, smacking her gum and tossing a thick braid over one shoulder.

"I'm fine," Kaitlin protested as Mara came around the counter and placed a hand on her shoulder.

"Scone or brownie?" the willowy brunette asked.

"Brownie."

Mara released Kaitlin long enough to pluck a cellophane-wrapped square from the basket next to the cash register, then led her to a high-top table in the corner.

"If you need chocolate this early, *fine* doesn't cut it."

Kaitlin didn't bother to argue even though it would make her late to work. Mara was the closest friend she had in town so Kaitlin wouldn't pretend everything was great.

She opened her mouth, unsure of how to explain the situation, but Mara held up a hand. "This is a two-bite story. I can tell."

"What does that mean?"

Elegant fingers unwrapped the brownie. "Two bites of chocolate and then you can start talking. It's emotional fortification. Trust me. I've been there."

With a soft laugh, Kaitlin took the hunk of brownie Mara handed to her. Although the dessert had been baked the previous day, it was still moist. She closed her eyes as she chewed, savoring the rich sweetness.

"This is your recipe," she said after swallowing. "It's way better than the brownies your aunt bakes."

Mara looked almost embarrassed at having her talent called out. "You don't even want to know how many late-night baking sessions I had after my divorce."

"I would have gained a hundred pounds," Kaitlin admitted.

Mara flashed a grin. "I took everything into Evie's day care. Those ladies were actually disappointed when I started to get myself together."

"I doubt that," Kaitlin said as she took a second

bite. "Okay, maybe I believe it," she amended as the chocolate hit her taste buds once again.

She'd met Mara almost a year ago, when the single mother had moved to Starlight and started working at Perk, as the locals called it. Kaitlin loved the fact that she'd become a part of this small community, even if a few people remained stand-offish due to her close relationship with Jack.

Mara's aunt, Nanci Morgan, owned Main Street Perk and had taken in Mara and her ador-able daughter when they'd moved to town. Appar-ently she'd gone through a nasty divorce that had decimated her, both emotionally and financially.

Kaitlin had immediately liked the snarky, sar-castic barista, as she had a sixth sense for rec-ognizing another wounded soul. Most people in Starlight had grown up in town or lived there for years, and she was grateful for a connection with someone who was also starting over.

Kaitlin was an only child and had found it dif-ficult to make close friends as a kid when she and her mom moved around so often. Cindi Carmody had a habit of falling fast and hard for whichever man caught her eye. Since she typically stuck to run-down, month-to-month rental apartments, she was always happy to shack up with a boy-friend as soon as he'd invite her into his home. The older Kaitlin got, the more her mom seemed to be scraping the bottom of the barrel with the men she chose. She had a penchant for pills and had been to rehab three times before Kaitlin had graduated high school.

Each time Kaitlin had been thrust into a different foster care family, and she'd hated and resented every experience.

She doubted Mara had ever sunk to the depths she'd experienced. Despite her reduced circumstances since the divorce, her friend retained a level of polish and class that came from having experienced a privileged life. Mara might be standoffish with people who didn't know her well, but she wasn't a snob, and she seemed to appreciate that Kaitlin didn't judge her for how far down in life she'd presumably tumbled.

"Okay, the chocolate should be hitting your system," Mara said with a wink as Kaitlin wiped one corner of her mouth with a paper napkin. "What's going on?"

"Trouble at work," Kaitlin said with a sigh and watched her friend blow out a relieved breath. "What did you think?"

"Your ex-boyfriend," Mara admitted. She was the only person in Starlight who knew about what a scumbag Robbie had been.

"No more man trouble for me," Kaitlin said, then bit her lip. "Well, not exactly."

"That sounds intriguing."

One word to describe Finn. *Irritating, irresistible* and *irate* also came to mind.

"Jack's son is in town," Kaitlin explained. "He found out about the cancer and the trouble at the bank. He blames me."

"For cancer?" Mara sounded outraged.

"No. Of course not. For what's happening at the bank." Over drinks at Mara's tiny bungalow a few weeks ago, Kaitlin had confided her fear that Jack's focus on his cancer treatment was compromising his ability to run the bank. She understood Jack didn't want anyone to know about his illness but had needed to share her worry with someone she trusted.

"Why would that be your fault?"

Kaitlin shrugged. "He had Nick Dunlap run a background check on me."

"You were wild but not exactly a white-collar criminal," Mara pointed out, her pert nose wrinkling.

"No doubt." Kaitlin sipped her coffee, the sweetness of the smoky caramel flavor soothing her like she was a child who'd been given a lollipop after skinning her knee on the playground.

"But it still has nothing to do with you."

"He also wants me to help him figure out a solution."

"He thinks you're part of the problem *and* he wants you on his team?" Mara glanced over her shoulder at the line forming around the side of the coffee bar.

"I'm guessing it's his version of 'keep your friends close but your enemies closer.'"

"You've done nothing wrong," Mara reminded her. "In fact, Finn has you to thank for his dad's recovery. Your research discovered the doctor working on the successful treatment."

The bells over the entrance tinkled, and like a moth to a flame, Kaitlin's attention was drawn to the tall, devastatingly handsome man entering the coffee shop.

Mara gave an appreciative whistle under her breath. "Tell me that's not Finn Samuelson."

Finn glanced toward their table, his blue eyes darkening when his gaze met Kaitlin's. She thought about the warmth of his finger on her cheek. The answering heat that had pooled low in her belly. Goose bumps pricked along her skin, and she dug her fingernails into the fleshy part of her palm, willing herself not to react. Finn's dark brows furrowed slightly. Then he nodded in greeting and headed to the back of the line.

"You see my problem, right?"

Kaitlin shifted her gaze across the table toward

her friend. Mara was fanning herself with one hand, a smile curving her lips.

"I saw the way he looked at you."

"Like I'm a criminal," Kaitlin muttered.

"Like he wants to do things to you that are probably illegal in a number of states," Mara answered with a laugh. "What happened to your self-imposed dry spell with dating?"

"It's still in effect."

Mara shook her head. "Then you'd better hope Finn's stay in Starlight is a short one. I'm not sure how anyone would resist that guy for long."

"It's not a matter of resisting," Kaitlin insisted. "He doesn't trust me."

"But he wants you," Mara told her, "and that's either better or worse depending on your perspective."

Kaitlin darted another glance at the way the tailored suit jacket stretched across Finn's broad shoulders as he waited in line. "Definitely worse," she whispered.

Mara stood and reached across to give her a quick hug. "I need to get back. Just remember that this is your home now. Don't let Finn Samuelson, or anyone, make you feel like you don't deserve the life you've created here."

"I didn't even tell you my fear," Kaitlin said with a strangled laugh, "and you knew it anyway."

"It's my gift," Mara said. She pointed a finger at Kaitlin. "And don't have sex with him. No complications."

"I would never in a million years…" Kaitlin trailed off. She absolutely would have taken Finn to bed, and not that long ago. In her old life she had a penchant for making bad decisions and self-sabotaging, often with bad choices in men. "I'm not planning to do anything with Finn."

"Stick to the plan," Mara said with a nod, then headed back to work.

Kaitlin popped one last bite of brownie into her mouth, then rewrapped the leftover bit and shoved it into her purse. She felt both calmer after talking to Mara and kind of jittery from the extra shot of caffeine.

Those jitters turned into a full-blown swarm of butterflies flitting across her stomach when she turned to find Finn waiting for her at Perk's entrance.

"Good morning," she said as she approached, proud of how calm her voice sounded. "You got through the line in record time."

He held up his cup. "Black coffee is an easy order. How did you sleep?" he asked, and she immediately choked on a swallow of coffee.

"Fine." She wiped at her mouth with the back of her hand.

He gave her a look like he knew she was lying. She'd always been a terrible liar, something that had probably kept her from getting into more trouble back in the day. It was difficult to take too many risks when she had no confidence in her ability to not get caught.

She imagined the amount of fun she could have getting caught by Finn.

"Your dad was still at the house when I left," she said, reminding them both of the connection between them. Not her physical reaction, which she needed to ignore.

"What time does he usually get to the office?"

"By nine."

He let out a disbelieving snort. "Some things never change. When we were kids, he was gone by sunup and often back late at night after a business dinner."

"He's not the same as he used to be," she said, widening her steps to match his as they crossed the street.

"I get it."

"Do you?" The entrance to the bank was two storefronts away, and Kaitlin took hold of Finn's muscled arm, moving to block his progress, much as she had when he'd shown up to see Jack yesterday.

"It's not just about the cancer," she clarified.

"You've been gone for years, Finn. I understand that you had problems with your father when you were younger, but he's not a villain. Whatever perceived grievances you have, I know he regrets not being closer to you and your sister."

"Perceived?" he repeated, temper turning his voice razor sharp. "You have no idea what my childhood was like or how he closed himself off after Mom died. It was like living with a ghost. He just faded away, only materializing when he wanted to yell at Ella or tell me how I needed to work harder to live up to the Samuelson legacy. The pressure of..." His eyes narrowed. "What is that?"

"You don't recognize it?" She'd raised her hands in front of her chest and cocked her head like she was playing a musical instrument. "It's the tiniest violin in the world with a song of great pity for your horrible childhood."

"You can't understand—"

"Give me a break." She stepped closer until the toes of her black high-heeled shoes just touched the fronts of his expensive-looking leather wingtips. "Look at this town." She spread her hands wide, careful not to spill her coffee. "It's like Washington's version of Pleasantville. It's tragic that your mom died and awful that your dad had trouble dealing with it." She dropped her arms. "But you can't convince me you didn't have it pretty good. Let's play a little game of 'have you ever,' Finnie-boy."

He looked at once annoyed and amused by the endearment.

Kaitlin drew in a deep breath, then asked, "Did you ever have to sneak food from the cafeteria trash can because there were no groceries in the house?"

He blinked. "Of course not."

"Ever get put into foster care when your parent went to rehab?"

"You know I didn't."

Old anger and bitterness swelled in her. She should push it down but instead let it wash over her like a wave, losing herself in all she'd endured even though it still hurt. "Have you ever sneaked out of your bedroom window and slept a night under the playground slide in your neighborhood park because your mom's lousy boyfriend of the week got that look in his eye when you were brushing your teeth?" A tremor went through her at the memory. "The look that said he was coming into your bedroom late that night and nothing was going to stop him."

"Kaitlin."

She shook off the sympathy in his tone. "You don't know hard."

His full mouth thinned and a crease appeared between his brows. "When I was fourteen, my mom had a seizure while driving me to football practice. I'd been in the middle of a teenage rant complaining because we were running five minutes late. She ran off the road and crashed into a tree. I was ejected from the car but sustained only minor injuries."

"I'm sorry for your loss," she whispered, "but—"

He held up a hand. "You said your piece. It's my turn." He ran the same hand through his hair and she noticed his fingers trembled. "The front of the car was like an accordion, collapsing into my mother and damaging her inner organs. I couldn't free her no matter how hard I tried. Another driver dialed 911 but she died before the ambulance arrived. I was holding her hand when she let go."

Reaching out, he traced a finger along the tears streaming down her cheeks. Kaitlin hadn't realized she was crying. "I don't think you want to weigh our respective situations and tally who had it worse. We both went through something terrible."

She gave a shaky nod, embarrassed that she'd gone down this road with him in the first place.

"It's great that you and my father are friends." Finn drew back his hand. "I appreciate everything you've done for him. But don't tell me I'm not entitled to my own feelings about my childhood. They're none of your business."

"Your dad has talked about you a lot in the past few months. He has a lot of regrets, Finn. I just wanted you to know that." Even to her own ears the rationale sounded weak.

"Duly noted. Now, stay out of my life."

Finn turned on his heel and stalked toward the bank, and Kaitlin felt like the biggest jerk on the planet.

Chapter Five

Two hours later, Finn massaged a hand along the back of his neck, still feeling like a colossal jerk for how he'd spoken to Kaitlin.

He also couldn't believe he'd shared so much detail of his mother's death. He hadn't talked about the accident for years. Of course, everyone who'd been in Starlight at the time knew what happened.

But if his family ever came up in conversation in Seattle, he said as little as possible. A few people knew his mother had died when he was in high school but no one knew the circumstances.

He hated the sharp ache in his gut that accompanied his memories. He hated himself for trying to one-up Kaitlin in the crappy-childhood department. She'd revealed a lot about herself with those "have you ever" questions, and the vulnerability in her melty brown eyes had triggered something in him. Something ugly and small that caused him to lash out.

He knew his childhood wasn't the worst. The car wreck that had claimed his mother's life was unthinkably tragic and an event no child—no person—should ever have to endure. But he'd known she loved him. Hell, she'd spent the last minutes of her life whispering words of comfort to him, telling him he was brave and strong and how proud she already was of the man she knew he'd become.

Despite the way his father had closed himself off emotionally after her death, he'd taken care of Finn and Ella. They might have wanted for affection but little else. There were a hell of a lot of levels on the hierarchy of need they'd had met, unlike Kaitlin.

No, Finn had endured tragedy but his life hadn't been tragic.

Maybe that was why he'd reacted so harshly. As much as he would have liked to blame his father or use the excuse of his mom's death for the vague discontent he couldn't shake, he understood deep inside that he was the one lacking. He was to blame. He'd been given so much more than most. Way more than Kaitlin with her laundry list of childhood horrors.

Yet he couldn't find happiness. His heart refused to settle. The longer he remained alone, the more certain he became that his heart was the real problem. Was he a real-life happiness grinch? The organ that beat inside his rib cage didn't exactly feel two sizes too small, more like frozen or stunted in its development.

Returning to Starlight seemed to highlight that fact. This town, with memories around every corner, made him feel in a way he'd forgotten he was capable of, and he hated that most of all.

It was safer on his own. His ordered, compartmentalized life suited him and the amount he was able to give. His plan had been to confront his father and gain confirmation that Finn could move on with his life. That he had a good reason for his hindered emotions. But the changes in his father and Kaitlin's affection for the old man prevented such an easy out.

Finn would never admit it, but he was jealous of Kaitlin's relationship with his dad, of her easy loyalty and the way Jack seemed to rely on her. The old man had been an emotional island since Finn's mom died, or at least that was Finn's impression. What if Finn had spent a decade stoking the fires of his anger and bitterness for no good reason?

He pushed away from the computer and stood. He'd been given space in an empty office now being used for storage. When Kaitlin arrived at the office, a few minutes after him and refusing to make eye contact, she'd introduced him to the personal bankers and tellers, explaining that he was working on a new investment project with his dad.

It had further embarrassed him when the bank's staff, both new and old, gave him an enthusiastic welcome. Several people mentioned that they felt like he was already a part of First Trust because of how proudly Jack spoke of him.

He'd seen Kaitlin's shoulders go stiff, as if she expected him to lash out at the suggestion that his father cared about him, the way he had with her.

She'd disappeared soon after, and he couldn't help but wonder if she'd purposely set him up with the space farthest from his dad's because she wanted to avoid him. That would be the smart choice for both of them, but Finn wasn't feeling wise at the moment.

The morning hadn't produced the proverbial smoking gun he'd expected, something that would clarify why the bank was struggling. Instead he'd discovered a simple but bleak explanation, a series of risky decisions and unfortunate circumstances combining in a perfect storm of plunging profits and excessive losses.

It seemed unfathomable that his dad had mismanaged the business so catastrophically. With a ball of unease festering in his gut, he left the office, making polite conversation with a few people as he headed down the hall.

Kaitlin gave him a tight nod as he passed her desk, and it was on the tip of his tongue to apologize. Then the door to his father's office opened, Jack emerging with a smile for his assistant that faded when he caught sight of Finn.

Typical.

"Satisfied your curiosity?" he demanded.

Finn shook his head. "The bank is headed for big problems if you don't address your overly aggressive lending and risky credit portfolio."

"Keep your voice down." Kaitlin leaned forward over her desk, checking the empty hallway to make sure no one had overheard him. "You know how fast gossip travels in a town like Starlight."

He did his best to ignore the way her breasts strained against the fabric of her thin sweater. He hadn't had this kind of uncontrolled reaction to a woman in…well…ever, that he remembered.

"It's fact," he told her, "not gossip."

"Then you and Jack will fix it."

His father scoffed. "There's nothing to fix. We've been doing business the same way for decades. Our model is solid and will see us through."

Could it be as simple as that? Was it possible his dad's unwillingness to modernize and his insistence on funding every loan application submitted by someone in the community had caused all of the issues he saw with the bottom line?

He refocused his attention as his dad pointed at him. "First Trust made it through the Great Depression and the banking crisis of 1933. We're still standing strong. Things can't be as bad as you're making them seem. We've had ups and downs before and we'll weather whatever comes our way."

Finn glanced at Kaitlin, who flashed the barest hint of a pleading smile, as if silently asking him to ignore his father's rant and help make things right.

"I'm driving over to Seattle," he announced, earning a frown from Kaitlin. "I'll be late tonight," he added. "I have a friend who's a banking analyst. I'd like him to check out the debt-to-income ratio and see if he has any ideas."

"You can't share our information with a stranger," his dad protested immediately.

"I have to if we're going to turn things around." He ran a hand through his hair. "Dad, the bank is your legacy. Even though I'm not involved, I can respect that. I don't want it to fail, and I know you don't, either. Too many people in Starlight depend on you. Please let me help."

His father's thick silver brows drew together. "Take Kaitlin with you," he said instead of responding directly to Finn's comments.

"What?" both he and Kaitlin asked at once.

Jack gestured toward Kaitlin. "I trust her."

"But not me?" Finn demanded.

"Finn can handle this," Kaitlin added.

Jack looked between the two of them. "I trust you both, and I want you working together."

"Dad, I don't think—"

"Besides," his father interrupted, "she works too much. Kaitlin could use a night out on the town in the big city."

"I don't like the city," she whispered, and Finn noticed the color had drained from her face.

"Use the corporate card. Dinner's on me."

"I'm not going to Seattle for fun," Finn protested.

"Would it kill you to have some?" Jack pointed to Kaitlin. "*You* definitely need some fun in your life."

"My life is plenty fun," she argued weakly.

Jack laughed. "The only way I'll agree to Finn continuing to have access to bank data is if the two of you become a team."

"I'm supposed to meet with the mayor's office to talk over the signage for the art fair."

"I'll handle it," Jack said. "I mean it about the access, Finn."

"Fine," he muttered.

"Not fine," Kaitlin shot back.

"Work it out," Jack said with a wave of his hand before disappearing back into this office.

"I'm not going to Seattle with you," Kaitlin said, her wide mouth pulled into a mulish line.

"You have to. You know my dad. He'll shut me out if I don't meet his terms."

"Why do those terms have to involve me?"

He shrugged. "Not a question I can answer." He checked the silver Rolex that encircled his wrist. "But it doesn't surprise me. It's why I asked you to help in the first place. We need to get going. I told Roger I'd be at his office by noon."

When she didn't move, he stepped forward. "It's one afternoon, Kaitlin. It won't be that bad. I promise."

She sat as still as stone for a moment longer, then reached into a desk drawer and yanked out her purse. "I'll drive along for the meeting, but dinner is unnecessary. We can come right back after you finish with your friend."

"Whatever you want," he said. "And, Kaitlin?"

She looked at him. "Yes?"

"I'm sorry about earlier and even sorrier about everything you went through as a kid."

Color bloomed in her cheeks. "I shouldn't have shared any of that."

"I'm glad you did," he said, surprised to find the statement so true. "It was good for me to have a reminder that as sad as my mom's death was, I was lucky to have her and to know she loved me."

She gave a small nod and then they headed out of the bank. Finn opened the passenger door to the BMW, taking a deep breath as she slipped in. This return trip to Starlight was becoming more complicated by the second.

Especially his feelings for Kaitlin.

As shocked as he'd been by his dad's suggestion that she join him in Seattle, he liked the idea of spending the afternoon with her. That could lead to nothing good for either of them.

"A town like Starlight is a big change after living in Seattle," Finn said as the landscape on either side of the highway changed from rugged to pastoral to urban.

"I needed the change." Kaitlin grasped her hands tightly in her lap.

They'd been driving close to an hour, and she had yet to relax. She'd made a clean break when she left Seattle. Although Finn was meeting his friend in the heart of downtown, nowhere near her old stomping grounds on the south side, nerves still danced across her stomach. Seattle was a great city, but her life there had been a mess. She didn't want any reminders of that this afternoon.

"Do you miss any part of it?"

"The water," she answered automatically. She had to give Finn credit for trying.

She understood he was as unhappy having her riding shotgun on this drive as she was to be with him. But he'd tried to keep up the guise of friendly conversation for most of the trip, although her anxiety prevented her from giving him more than basic answers to his questions.

She drew in a breath and forced her body to relax. "I used to save my money to take the ferry to Bainbridge Island. The lakes around Starlight are nice, but it's not the same."

He nodded. "I bought a boat with my first bonus check."

"Of course you did," she said with a soft laugh, as if she needed another reminder of how different their lives were.

"It was small," he added, almost sheepishly. "The first time I took it out, the engine died and I couldn't figure out how to fix it. The coast guard had to come and tow me back to the dock."

She grinned and couldn't help but appreciate

that he'd shared the memory with her. "At least tell me you weren't wearing a captain's hat and an ascot."

"Only in my mind."

"I assume you got better at the whole sea-captain vibe."

He shrugged, and she noticed his fingers tighten on the steering wheel. "I sold it a couple of years ago. I didn't have the time for it."

"You're a classic workaholic."

"There are expectations when you're on the senior management track."

"Expectations are the worst," she said softly, and Finn laughed. The sound landed like a fist to her chest, stealing her breath.

She could tell herself all day long that she hadn't wanted to go to Seattle because of her past, but a part of her was afraid of spending time with him. Terrified of the way he made her feel and the unexpected connection joining them when they were together.

More quality time was exactly what she didn't need with this man.

"My dad said you were overdue for some fun." He glanced over at her before exiting the interstate toward downtown. "Does that mean you're a workaholic?"

"I'm just boring," she admitted.

He laughed again. "I doubt that."

"Don't get me wrong. I like it that way. Starlight is a good fit for me. The town rolls up the sidewalks early most nights, and I'm already home and tucked into bed with a good book."

"Just a book?" The car pulled to a stop at a red light, and Finn lifted a brow as he looked at her again. "No boyfriend to help you turn the pages?"

"I can turn the pages just fine on my own," she told him, color flooding her cheeks when she realized the not-so-subtle innuendo of their conversation.

"Duly noted," he said, his voice taking on a hoarse tone.

"It must be difficult for you to be away from work. I get the impression it doesn't happen often."

"I have a client I take skiing down in Lake Tahoe over the holidays. That's the only vacation I've had in years."

"Entertaining a client isn't vacation."

"It's me not in the office."

"Still doesn't count," she insisted, reaching over to poke his arm.

"Ouch."

A giggle bubbled up in her throat, and she clamped her mouth shut. "You're a baby."

"Am not." He squeezed her leg just above her knee and she squirmed. "You're boy crazy."

"Oh, heck, no." She grabbed his hand, smiling at the old childhood test. "Used to be, but not anymore."

But when she went to release him, he turned his hand, lacing his fingers with hers. "I'm glad you came with me."

"Why?" she couldn't help but ask.

"I don't want to be alone right now," he said, his fingers tightening on hers.

Kaitlin swallowed as emotion washed through her. Sometimes it felt like she'd been alone most of her life. For this man to want her with him meant something, even if she desperately didn't want it to.

"What do you think your friend will tell you?"

Finn gave a slight shake of his head. "I don't know. My hope is that he sees something that I'm missing in the financials I emailed. Something that offers an easy explanation for how to fix things."

"And if the answer isn't an easy one?"

He released her hand. "Another question I can't answer."

"The bank means the world to your father."

"It became his whole life after Mom died, even more than it was before."

"You and your sister mean more."

He let out a snort as he maneuvered into a parking space on a busy street a few blocks from the water.

Although she'd grown up in Seattle, Kaitlin hadn't spent much time in this part of the city. Businesspeople and trendy hipsters crowded the street. Even though she wore an outfit that was totally professional in Starlight, here she felt underdressed and out of place.

She got out of Finn's sleek car and waited while he fed the meter. When he glanced up at her, all the teasing from a few minutes earlier had disappeared from his blue gaze. Although he and his father were estranged, she could tell how much he wanted to get the bank back on track as a way to potentially mend his relationship with Jack.

She followed him into the modern office building, hoping for good news for both him and his dad.

Chapter Six

"This can't come as a surprise. We see it far too often in community banks. First Trust has been overly aggressive in lending, and now the debt-to-income ratio is way off." Roger Franks removed his reading glasses and leveled a sympathetic look toward Finn. "You didn't really think there was a smoking gun in these financials?"

Finn forced his reeling mind to focus. Roger might be confirming what Finn already knew, but he'd held out some slim hope that there was another explanation. He could feel the weight of Kaitlin's shocked stare on him but didn't turn toward her.

"No," he admitted quietly. "But I hoped you'd find something I missed."

Roger let out a small laugh. "When was the last time you missed something, Samuelson?"

Finn pressed two fingers to his temple. His head was pounding. "Never."

"Your family's bank is nearing the verge of failure."

"Can it be saved?"

Roger put his glasses on again and turned his attention back to the computer screen. "Maybe," he said after a moment. "But it would be easier to find a buyer. First Trust has one of two bank charters issued in Starlight. You know how valuable that is, Finn. AmeriNat specializes in this sort of deal. Your division specifically. If you got in touch with—"

"No," Finn interrupted. "I know my dad won't agree to sell."

"It would kill him," Kaitlin whispered.

Finn wanted her to be wrong. His father had survived the death of his soul mate and estrangement from both of his kids and had just kicked cancer's butt to the curb. But the bank was different. It wasn't just something his father loved. First Trust was a big part of who his dad was. His identity. His legacy.

And it was failing.

"I need a plan," Finn said, more to himself than to either Roger or Kaitlin.

Roger leaned back in his chair. "This isn't your wheelhouse, Finn. You're a regional director with one of the largest financial institutions in the country. Your focus is growth metrics, not running a family bank."

Finn had met Roger Franks his senior year of college, when he'd interned at the company where Roger was a senior partner. The older man had become both a mentor and a friend over the years, as well as a cautionary tale. Roger was a genius when it came to banking, but he'd also just finalized a divorce from his third wife. Finn had known walking down the aisle again was a mistake, but Roger insisted on chasing his own happily-ever-after even though his true love remained his career. No one and nothing could take its place.

The two of them had a lot in common, but Finn didn't want to believe that single-minded focus on work was something they shared. He had very few examples of happy marriages in his life. His parents' union had been one of them. His dad had always worked long hours, but he'd loved Finn's mother with his whole heart. And that had made it all the more difficult when his dad closed down so completely after her death. It was as if Finn and Ella weren't worthy of love with their mother gone.

Now the one love Jack had left was in jeopardy.

Finn shook his head, unsure why he felt such a desire to fix this but needing to do it just the same. "It doesn't matter. Tell me what to do."

Roger's bushy brows drew down over his eyes. "The bank needs to modernize. Draw in new customers while keeping the old ones happy with the personalized service they offer. Most important, they need to be more cautious with lending and minimize the risk for the bank's credit portfolio."

"How long will it take?"

"You need to implement some of these strategies immediately. Sooner if possible. If the bank can bring in new depositors quickly, you may have a chance at righting things."

Panic and resignation battled deep inside him. He didn't have six months, or even six weeks, to devote to his family's bank. How was he supposed to put his life on hold? But if he didn't, would his dad lose everything?

As if sensing his mounting anxiety, Roger gave him an encouraging smile. "I have a plan we put together for a community bank outside Portland. They didn't have quite the same set of issues but close enough that it may help." He looked from Finn to Kaitlin. "Maybe there's someone you trust in Starlight to spearhead this for you."

Finn heard a soft scoff and kept his gaze on Roger. "I'll figure it out. Thanks for everything."

He stood, still not willing to look at Kaitlin. He couldn't stand it if he saw doubt in her eyes. Even with Roger's ideas, Finn knew his bid to turn things around was a long shot.

"I hear wedding bells might be in your future," Roger said, almost as an afterthought, as he walked them toward the door.

Finn stopped so suddenly that Kaitlin bumped into him. She quickly stepped away as he turned toward Roger. "I'm not even dating anyone at the moment."

The older man clapped him on the shoulder. "I golfed last week with Peter. We saw Chelsea's father in the clubhouse. Ray said the two of you were taking a break."

Another sharp pain erupted behind Finn's right eye. He'd met his ex-girlfriend, Chelsea Davidson, at a charity event he'd attended with a client. Her dad was a prominent attorney in Seattle and close friends with Peter Henry, his bank's chief operating officer. On paper she was his perfect match and they'd dated for almost a year. He never should have let it go on that long, but she made it too easy for him. Chelsea had never seemed to expect anything from him until he realized the one thing she did want was an engagement ring. He couldn't give her that, even though he knew it would help his bid for a promotion.

"We aren't together," he told Roger but somehow knew it was Kaitlin he wanted to hear those words. "The relationship ended for good."

Roger rolled his eyes. "Not if Peter and Ray have anything to say about it. Those two were plotting like a couple of matchmaking mamas."

"No wedding bells," Finn insisted, the words coming out a low growl.

"Whatever you say." Roger turned to Kaitlin. "It was lovely to meet you."

As the two shook hands, Finn darted a glance in her direction. If the news of his ex-girlfriend affected her in any way, she hid it well. Not that she should be affected. Or that he wanted her to be. Except...

He left the office and strode toward his car, leaving Kaitlin to catch up to his long strides. He clicked the button on his key fob to unlock the BMW's doors and slid behind the wheel. As soon as the passenger door closed, he pulled away from the curb, focusing all his energy on maneuvering through downtown traffic.

He turned after a few blocks and entered the parking garage under the building that housed his condo. He waited for Kaitlin to speak, but she remained silent, as if she somehow understood he was at his breaking point right now. He never imagined being in this position with his father.

She followed as he got out after parking, and the sound of their shoes on the concrete echoed through the cool, quiet space. He punched the elevator button, and the doors slid open. It could be any normal day, although he wouldn't usually return home in the early afternoon. But the action of pulling out his keys and heading down the hall on the seventh floor, where his condo was located felt so routine. If he concentrated only on the moment, he could almost pretend his life hadn't been turned upside down.

But pretending wouldn't help anyone.

"Nice place," Kaitlin said quietly, and Finn glanced around his condo like he was seeing it for the first time.

He'd bought it for the location and because the address fit with his image. He hadn't given much thought to the decor. Any thought, really, since he'd hired an interior designer the firm used to buy all of his furniture. She'd gone for a typical bachelor look of sleek leather couches and contemporary accents.

It had seemed fine at the time, but he had to admit he didn't have one comfortable place to sit other than his king-size bed. Best not to think about his bed and Kaitlin at the same time.

He loosened his tie as he walked into the kitchen. "You really think so?" he asked, pulling two glasses out of a cabinet.

"If you're into sterile waiting rooms as design inspiration," she said dryly, "this place is the bomb."

Despite the tension rolling through him, Finn smiled at her smart-aleck comment. Kaitlin Carmody didn't pull any punches, and her refreshing honesty was damn attractive.

"Let me guess." He turned and placed the glasses on the island that now separated them, then reached into a lower cabinet for a bottle of liquor. "You're into lace doilies and embroidered throw pillows?"

One side of her mouth kicked up. "You might benefit from a needlepoint pillow around here. Maybe with the message 'Trust me. I'm a banker.'"

"I'll keep that in mind the next time I'm out shopping."

He poured a finger of liquor into each glass, then pushed one toward her.

"Liquid lunch?"

"Liquid and then lunch," he clarified. "It's been that kind of a morning."

She picked up the glass, grimacing as she sniffed the scotch.

"That's an eighteen-year-old single-malt scotch."

"Still smells like lighter fluid if you ask me," she told him but took a tiny sip as he downed his.

"Not much of a drinker," he said when they'd both placed their glasses back on the counter, his empty and hers still filled.

"Not anymore." She hugged her arms around her waist. "Back in the day I could have drunk you under the table." She tapped one finger on the rim of the glass. "Even then I didn't like the taste. But temporarily obliterating reality made downing copious amounts of cheap booze worth it."

The more time he spent with Kaitlin, the more difficult it was to imagine her as a hard-partying wild child. Her presence grounded him, and he couldn't imagine her ever losing control. He had to admit he would have liked to see her lose control. Not with alcohol but from his touch.

Shaking his head, he undid the top two buttons of his shirt, then grabbed two water bottles from the refrigerator.

"This might be more your speed," he said as he handed her one.

She nodded and took it from him, her fingers grazing his.

"What are we doing here, Finn?"

"I need to pack," he answered simply.

She took a drink of water, then pressed her lips together. "How long will you stay in Starlight?"

He liked that she didn't pretend not to understand his intention. "Like I said, I haven't taken a real vacation in years. I can get some time off. My boss won't like it, but I'll be able to manage most of the day-to-day business remotely."

"How long?"

He blew out a breath. "A couple of weeks."

She closed her eyes for a moment. "Thank you," she whispered.

"I don't know if it will be enough," he admitted. "But if I can manage to implement some of the initiatives Roger mentioned…"

"I'll help in whatever way you need. Everyone at First Trust will pitch in. No one wants to see the bank fail."

Finn eyed the bottle of whiskey. Of course it wouldn't help the situation to get totally drunk, but it would certainly feel good in the moment. He grabbed the bottle and shoved it back into the cabinet before he made a decision he'd certainly regret. "What about my father?"

"Jack wants the bank to do well. You can't think otherwise."

"I know he's dedicated, but you have to understand that First Trust is in this situation because he wouldn't modernize and he won't say no to anyone who needs money. As much as I wanted there to be a smoking gun or a villain—"

"Me," she interrupted.

He inclined his head. "I apologize for that. But yes, I wanted you… Doug, who smells like onions… Anyone to blame for all of the problems. A bad guy is easier to vanquish than an old man so stuck in his ways that he runs his own business into the ground."

"Doug *always* smells like onions," she said, wrinkling her nose. "No matter what time of day it is. That's weird, right?"

He laughed again. "It's kind of nasty."

Her features softened, as if it made her happy to hear him laugh. God help him, he liked the idea of making this woman happy.

"We can convince your father to make the changes," she promised. "I know it." She reached across the island and squeezed his hand. Her fingers were warm, her touch comforting. When was the last time someone had comforted him? When had he ever allowed it?

He looked down at her small hand covering his. Emotion gathered in the back of his throat and he pulled away.

"I was a jerk to you."

She flashed a crooked smile. "I understand why Doug had suspicions. I became pretty protective of your dad during the cancer treatments, and no one understood the reason. Of course, I also figured you were a jerk in general."

"That could be."

"It doesn't matter." She waved her hand as if dismissing his rudeness, which bothered him. He got the impression she'd dealt with more than her fair share of disrespect and managed it far too easily.

"I'm sorry."

"Oh." Her mouth formed the syllable on a small puff of breath. Clearly she also wasn't accustomed to hearing those words. "Okay. Well, it's fine. Really."

He wanted to argue but could tell his attention to this detail bothered her. That was the last thing he wanted. To be honest, he needed Kaitlin's belief that the mess at the bank could be fixed. Even if she was faking her faith in him, it meant something. More than was smart for either of them.

"I'm going to change clothes and pack a couple of suitcases. I need more than I brought for the funeral." He pointed to the flat-screen TV that dominated the far wall of the condo. "Feel free to watch a show or whatever."

"Whatever," she echoed.

"We can get something to eat on the way back if you want."

"You don't need to do that," she told him. "I know your dad said I need to have more fun, but—"

"I need fun." He shrugged. "And food. You don't want to see me when I don't get three squares a day."

"Then you're a meal behind," she said, glancing at her watch.

"Exactly." He placed a hand to his stomach. "I'll be ready in five."

Running a hand through his hair, he walked toward his bedroom. He grabbed two oversize suitcases from the corner of the closet and began tossing in clothes. No need to bother with his best suits. Even at the bank, he'd be overdressed in Starlight. He shoved in as many clothes as he could fit, a few pairs of shoes, including his old and recently underused hiking boots, then pulled the two pieces of luggage back toward the main living area of the condo.

Kaitlin stood to one side of the sink, using a dish towel to dry the whiskey glasses. As he watched, she returned the clean glasses to the cabinet, folded the towel and set it on the counter.

"You didn't have to do that." He felt oddly touched by the small display of domesticity.

"I have an idea for our late lunch," she told him. "Or early dinner. Whatever you want to call it."

"Is it fun?"

"Yes, unless you're a stodgy, sanctimonious stick-in-the-mud."

He barked out a surprised laugh. "No pressure."

"Exactly," she agreed. She walked forward and wrapped her fingers around the handle of his smaller suitcase. "Let's go."

The small gesture of solidarity caused a faint pinch in his chest, somewhere in the vicinity of his heart. They walked to the parking garage in companionable silence and loaded the trunk with his luggage.

"You're confident you can get the time off from work?"

He shrugged and hit the button to turn on the car. "Yes, but it wouldn't change my decision if not. I have to do this. We both know it."

She punched something into her phone, then hit a button, and the GPS gave him instructions for which way to turn out of the parking lot.

"Are you going to tell me where we're headed?"

"On an adventure," she said, brown eyes dancing.

Adventure. Finn rolled the word around in his head for a moment. It felt unfamiliar and slightly terrifying. His life was about order and stability, and he was heading back into the murky waters of life in Starlight. He wasn't sure that counted as adventure or if his nerves could handle anything more right now. But Kaitlin was beautiful and smiling at him like she really wanted to spend this afternoon together, despite what an ass he'd been.

She was giving him a second chance, and he might not be the sharpest knife in the drawer but he was smart enough not to turn it away.

"Where you lead," he told her as he pulled out into the shockingly sunshiny Seattle day, "I'll follow."

Chapter Seven

Nerves danced across Kaitlin's stomach as Finn turned his fancy car onto the dusty gravel driveway twenty minutes later. They weren't far from downtown, but it might have been a different planet.

"Since when is there an amusement park in Seattle?" he asked, leaning over the steering wheel to take in the tall Ferris wheel, twisty roller coaster and various other festival rides.

"It's a traveling fair," Kaitlin said and bit down on her lower lip. "They've been open in this location every June for as long as I can remember."

"Seriously?" He glanced over at her. "I had no idea. Is this the part of town where you grew up?"

She swallowed. "Mostly," she admitted, knowing how shabby this area must seem compared to his upscale building or the sprawling rancher that was the Samuelson family home in Starlight. "I moved around a lot. Foster care and all that. But this was close enough that my friends and I could ride our bikes here on summer afternoons."

"That must have been awesome," Finn said, maneuvering the car over a deep rut in the pasture to park between two Ford trucks. "The most we had was a dunk booth at the town Independence Day festival."

"Your life in Starlight was perfect," she chided. "Don't try to tell me any different."

"Would you believe I've never been on a Ferris wheel?"

"Come on. What about the one on the waterfront downtown?"

"Not once."

"Then I'm glad we're here."

She unclipped her seat belt and reached for the door handle.

Finn placed a gentle hand on her arm, and she turned to find him grinning from ear to ear. "Me, too."

Warmth spread through Kaitlin, and she forced

herself to climb out of the car before she did something really stupid like launch herself across the console and into his lap.

She had no idea why she'd thought to bring him here in the first place. But ever since Jack had said she needed to have fun, Kaitlin had been thinking about the last time she'd associated that word with her life. The MegaFun Amusement Park had sprung to her mind. No matter what had been going on in her life during any given year, summer nights spent stuffing her face with cotton candy and running from ride to ride with her friends always made her forget.

Finn needed to forget everything going wrong in his life, at least for a few hours.

And the fact that he'd never been on a Ferris wheel confirmed that she'd made the right decision. As much as she wanted to keep her distance from him, even more she wanted to see him patch up his relationship with Jack. Maybe he'd even choose to stay in Starlight. She knew that was his father's dearest wish.

One step at time.

"I haven't been here for a few years," she told him as they approached the ticket booth. "But if it's the same as it used to be, we can start with a few ride tickets or get an all-access band. Either way—"

"Kaitlin."

She turned, frowning as Finn stared at her in disbelief, his muscular arms crossed over his chest. He'd changed from his suit into a casual olive green collared shirt and loose jeans, but he still looked out of place amid the couples and families walking past. With his expensive haircut, chunky designer watch on his wrist and general air of superiority, he clearly wasn't part of this world. Her world. The one she'd belonged to for so long.

"What's wrong?"

"Do I look like the kind of guy who'd be satisfied with a few tickets?"

"Um…is that a trick question?"

He chuckled. "Sweetheart, I'm all access all the time."

The way his mouth curved up, she could tell he was joking, but heat still gathered low in her belly at his gentle teasing. She could easily imagine what it would be like to give all access to a man like Finn.

All night long.

They ordered corn dogs and slushies as they walked around the fair, and then purchased wristbands and headed toward the first ride. The park wasn't as crowded as it would be later, but a few groups still stood in line in front of the brightly colored Ferris wheel.

"Why do they keep stopping with people at the top?" Finn rubbed a hand along the back of his neck as he gazed up at the ride.

"It's part of the fun," she told him, laughing when he gave her a look like she might be crazy. "Don't tell me you're afraid of heights."

"Of course not," he said too quickly.

"Right," she agreed. "A man like you isn't afraid of anything."

"Oh, I'm afraid of plenty," he answered, still studying the Ferris wheel. They shuffled forward in line as the older man operating the controls loaded groups on and off. "Going back to Starlight. Losing my family's bank. Torpedoing my career with this extended vacation. The potential fallout from wanting to kiss you so badly I can hardly think of anything else."

She drew in a sharp breath, shocked by both his honesty and what he'd said about wanting to kiss her.

"You're trying to distract me."

"Or myself," he countered.

Suddenly the ride operator motioned them to load into the empty passenger car.

When Finn didn't move, Kaitlin took his hand and led him forward. "One step at a time."

"This isn't so bad," he whispered as they rose

about twenty feet off the ground, then stopped while another car loaded below them.

"I used to love the Ferris wheel most of all." She started to release her grip on his hand when she realized she still held it. But Finn tugged her closer, draping an arm over her shoulder.

"Why?" he asked.

"Because for a few minutes I was on top of the world."

"Quite a sensation." His voice sounded slightly strangled as the Ferris wheel gave a shudder and they began to spin.

"You can see downtown from here," she said, pointing north. "Maybe you can pick out your building."

When Finn didn't answer, Kaitlin glanced toward him, then grimaced. His eyes were closed, his shoulders rigid, and his free hand gripped the metal bar like he was holding on for dear life.

"Are you okay?"

"I lied," he said through clenched teeth. "I'm totally afraid of heights."

She brushed the hair away from her face as the Ferris wheel rose and fell again. She loved the breeze and the view and everything about the ride.

"I can get the guy to stop it so we can get off."

Finn gave a sharp shake of his head. "I'm not admitting that to anyone but you."

She pressed two fingers to her chest when it pinched. Something about seeing this strong alpha male's vulnerable side made every one of her defenses start to disintegrate.

Inching closer, she wrapped her arm around his waist. "I've got you," she told him. "It's all going to be just fine."

That teased a bit of a smile from him. A smile that disappeared when they abruptly stopped at the very top of the ride.

"What the hell…" he muttered.

"Remember, it's part of the fun," she promised. "Look around."

He kept his gaze fixed on hers. "No way."

"Finn, it's amazing." She turned to look behind her, where she knew she'd be able to see Puget Sound in the distance. Her movement caused the car to sway.

Finn muttered a hoarse curse as he gripped her shoulders. "Don't move."

"We're fine," she assured him with a confident smile. "I told you I'd give you an adventure."

"You're going to give me a heart attack," he countered, closing his eyes again.

His chest hitched in shallow breaths and she could see a thin sheen of sweat along his hairline. *Oh, gah.* Kaitlin had planned to take his mind off his troubles and instead she was serving up a different kind of stress.

"I'm sorry," she whispered, placing her hand on his cheek. "I didn't know…"

"It's a stupid fear," he said through gritted teeth. "I can manage a ski lift so I figured I'd be okay on this thing. I *am* okay. Seriously."

He didn't look anywhere near okay to Kaitlin. The Ferris wheel jerked and they moved one car length forward, rocking gently as the ride stopped again.

A muscle in Finn's jaw clenched, and without letting herself think about what she was going to do, Kaitlin leaned in and brushed her lips over his. He didn't react for a moment but then angled his head so that their mouths joined more fully. Even with the breeze picking up, she could smell the scent of him—shampoo and some spicy cologne. It had been a long time since her body had reacted to a man the way it did to Finn. A long time since she'd allowed herself to act on any sort of physical attraction.

In truth, she doubted she could have prevented this moment. She'd wanted to kiss Finn Samuelson since the moment she'd looked up from her desk to find him glaring down at her. Which was stupid and self-destructive, two things Kaitlin hadn't allowed herself to be since moving to Starlight.

He deepened the kiss, seeming not to notice when the ride started, then stopped again. At least she was distracting him. And herself. This was safe, she rationalized. An innocent kiss out in public. She could get it out of her system, then go back to ignoring him. Her reaction probably had more to do with a two-year dry spell in the bedroom department than something specific to this man. Sure. That was the ticket. A couple minutes of kissing and she'd be done.

As Finn's grip on her shoulders gentled, he made a soft sound low in his throat, or maybe the noise came from her. Either way it lit her insides on fire, like a spark to a dry field. His kiss was incendiary and she'd never felt so willing to go up in flames.

She pressed closer and his fingers trailed along her collarbone, the touch featherlight but affecting her to her core.

Suddenly a chorus of wolf whistles and applause broke out around them. Kaitlin drew back, color flooding her cheeks when she realized they'd come to the end of the ride. The Ferris wheel operator stared at them, tapping an impatient foot on the metal stairs.

"You two didn't get it out of your systems in high school?" he asked with a dismissive snicker.

"Sorry," Kaitlin mumbled, scrambling out of

the car. She straightened her thin sweater as she walked off the platform, not making eye contact with anyone waiting in line.

As soon as they were around the corner, she glanced back at Finn, and they both dissolved into fits of laughter.

"Totally busted," Finn said, shaking his head.

"Did you see the mom with the two little girls?" Kaitlin grimaced. "She was sending me death glares. Her kids are probably scarred for life."

"It was a kiss," he answered. "More likely the mom was jealous."

"No doubt," she agreed. "That was a heck of a kiss."

Finn grinned, then made a show of looking around at the other rides. "I need to find something else really high up. I like how you distract me."

She gave him a playful shove. "That was a one-time deal."

He took her hand and drew her closer, winding his arms around her waist. "I hope not."

"Finn." She bit down on her lower lip. "We can't. You know we can't."

His expression turned mulish. "Why not?"

"It will overcomplicate an already complicated situation."

He leaned in, pressing his forehead to hers. "For a few minutes when I was scared of plummeting to my death in a freak amusement park accident, I actually forgot about everything else."

"That was the point of this."

"I thought you were just looking for an excuse to have your merry way with me."

She choked out a laugh. "I don't have a *merry* way."

"Liar," he whispered but stepped back from her. "What's next?"

"We're keeping you close to the ground," she told him, earning an eye roll.

"How about bumper cars?"

"Perfect."

He reached out and smoothed a stray lock of hair from her face. "Yeah, it is."

Her breath caught in her throat. The way he was looking at her made her feel…everything.

"I'm going to kick your butt in the bumper cars," she said, forcing a light tone. She had to keep this casual. It was a fun afternoon of blowing off steam. Nothing more.

"We'll see about that," he said as they headed toward the next ride.

They went on the bumper cars, the scrambler and then the merry-go-round. Finn won her a stuffed elephant at a game booth along the midway, and then they ate a dessert of sweet funnel cakes.

As the sun began to set, the fairgrounds glowed with thousands of twinkle lights. Kaitlin felt grimy and stuffed and happier than she could remember in ages.

Finn was like a little boy making up for lost time. Although they stayed away from a second ride on the Ferris wheel, he insisted on trying everything else. He was playful and flirty, and while they didn't kiss again, attraction continued to simmer between them.

By the time they were heading toward the exit, Kaitlin felt dizzy, both from the rides and the unexpected connection she felt with Finn. It was more than physical. She enjoyed him. She liked who she was with him, which was new for her with a man.

"I'm going to wash my hands before we leave," she said, holding them up, palms out. "I still feel sticky from the funnel cake sugar."

"Isn't sticky part of the fun?" he teased.

Oh, sure. It was going to be simple to go back to ignoring her feelings for him.

She made a show of rolling her eyes and shoved the elephant he'd won for her toward him. "Hold Josiah," she told him.

His brows furrowed. "Who names a stuffed elephant Josiah?"

"Me." She stuck out her tongue as he took the animal from her, then turned on her heel and flounced toward the bathroom. It had been years since Kaitlin had done any flouncing, but she couldn't help adding some extra swing in her hips. Finn's laughter echoed behind her as she entered the restroom.

She moved in front of the row of faucets, glancing up at herself as the water automatically began to flow.

Her cheeks were flushed and although her hair was messy and tangled and her makeup had given up the ghost hours earlier, she couldn't help but notice that she looked happy. Like she used to feel at the amusement park when she was a girl.

Why was happiness so underrated in adulthood?

Or perhaps just difficult to attain.

She concentrated on her hands as the door to the restroom opened.

"I thought that was you, Kait."

Kaitlin glanced up into the mirror to find Cammie Pruitt staring at her, a smile on her face more suited to a cat that'd just made a meal of the canary. All those happy memories dissolved like spun sugar on her tongue. Cammie had been a part of Kaitlin's life when the perception of popularity became more important than her true friends.

"It's me," she said, trying to sound casual. A quick check of her reflection as she turned for a paper towel showed her she was doing a terrible job of looking casual. "It's been a while. You look good, Cammie."

"Been a while?" The voluptuous blonde let out a shrill cackle. "You disappeared."

"I moved," Kaitlin corrected. "Not the same thing."

"Same result." Cammie sidled closer. "I saw the guy you're with tonight. Moving up in the world, huh?"

"He's a friend." Kaitlin crumpled the paper towel in her fist and commanded herself to get a grip. She could not show Cammie how rattled this impromptu reunion made her.

"With benefits, I hope."

"*Just* a friend." She turned and pasted a bland smile on her face. "What are you doing here? The rides always made you queasy."

Cammie nodded as she placed one hand on her hip. "My new guy has a kid who wanted to come. I'm auditioning for the role of loving stepmom."

"Good luck… I guess."

"Yeah, he's a rung up from the old neighborhood." She waggled her overly sculpted brows. "Not the colossal leap you made, but that's no surprise. You were always different from the rest of us. Better in some way."

Kaitlin swallowed. "I never thought I was better than anyone."

"Robbie did. It's why he picked you in the first place." Her hip jutted out and Kaitlin could all but feel the attitude being sent her way. "He was so angry when you left."

"We weren't good for each other. Everyone knew it."

"Not him."

"It's been two years," Kaitlin said helplessly.

"Oh, he's moved on," Cammie said with a snarky little laugh. "Plenty of times." She took a step closer. "But I'm sure he'd like to see you."

Panic gripped Kaitlin. Robbie had never been abusive, but they were toxic together. That whole part of her life had been poison. A complete break was the only way she could have extricated herself from their self-destructive codependency. And she might be different now but she had no intention of testing her resolve.

She'd left Robbie and Cammie and the hot mess she'd been far behind.

"That's not a great idea."

"So, where are you living now?" Cammie asked, the calculating light in her eyes belying her casual tone.

"On the north end of town," Kaitlin said, and it

wasn't totally a lie. The Samuelson property was on the north side of Starlight.

Cammie's eyes narrowed. "You're still in Seattle?"

"I'm in Seattle." That wasn't exactly a lie, either. She was in Seattle. At the moment. And planning to get the hell out of town as fast as possible. "It was great to see you." Now, that was a lie. "I hope things go well with your guy."

"Yours, too," Cammie said, moving aside so Kaitlin could pass.

"He's not mine," she said over her shoulder.

"In that case, you want to introduce me?" Cammie laughed at her own joke, but Kaitlin didn't bother to respond.

"Let's go," she said to Finn, who was waiting near the ticket booth.

She didn't wait for his answer but took long strides toward the parking lot, head down like someone else from her past might recognize her. She hadn't ever gone to the fair as an adult, so she wasn't expecting to see anyone she knew.

But if Cammie was here because of her boyfriend's kid, Kaitlin imagined others in her former circle of friends might have settled down. She'd only been gone two years, and this wasn't exactly the place for a baby or toddler, but still…

Finn caught up with her in a few steps. "What's the hurry?"

"Nothing. I just want to get back. An escape from reality is great, but tomorrow the real work starts. We can't be bleary-eyed for it."

"Are you worried about a funnel cake hangover?"

"That's not a thing."

It was easy to find the BMW in the sea of cars that filled the field. The sleek black sports car stuck out like a sore thumb, or more like a fine piece of silver on a table filled with plastic cutlery.

Just as she got to the passenger door, Finn placed a hand on her arm. "Kaitlin, what's going on?"

She spun toward him, ready to snap, but stopped abruptly when he held out the stuffed elephant.

"Josiah," she whispered, unable to prevent her smile. She wouldn't allow Cammie or anyone else to ruin this day. She'd spent so much of her life living in fear, doing nothing more than reacting to what other people did or said to set her off. It was easy to think she'd changed since her move to Starlight, but how much had she truly grown as a person if a few snide remarks from someone she used to know could put her back to square one?

"Terrible name for an elephant," Finn muttered but she could hear the amusement in his tone.

"I saw someone I used to know," she admitted. "From before I left Seattle."

"Not a friend, I take it."

"She had been a friend of a sort. We hung out in the same crowd." She swallowed, then said, "For a while, we dated guys who were best friends, so Cammie and I were together a lot."

"The boyfriend you left behind."

"Yeah." The word was no more than a whoosh of breath, a piece of dandelion fuzz carried along on the breeze.

"Regrets?"

"Too many to count," she admitted. "But none about walking away. It was just…disconcerting." She shrugged. "I grew up around here but forgot about the possibility of running into my past. I thought it would be fun. I didn't think much beyond that."

"I had fun," he said, and although his gaze darkened, he didn't move to touch her.

As much as she wanted him to, she appreciated that he held back. She wasn't sure her emotions could handle anything more at the moment.

"I'm glad. I did, too."

He nodded and opened the door for her. "Then it was a good day."

She smiled as she climbed into the car. A good day.

That would work for her.

Chapter Eight

"You're welcome here as long as you want."

Finn dropped his duffel bag to the tile floor of Nick's kitchen, then picked up the mug of coffee his friend had set on the counter for him. It had been three days since he and Kaitlin spent the afternoon in Seattle. He'd returned to his friend's house but didn't feel right bunking here for his entire stay in town.

"I appreciate that, but if part of the reason for returning to Starlight is making things better with my dad, it makes sense that I stay with him."

Nick studied him over the rim of his mug, which

read "Police officers do it with handcuffs." "Is that part of your reason?"

Finn grimaced as the bitter coffee hit his tongue. "I thought a cop would be able to make a better brew."

"I like it strong."

"There's strong…" Finn placed his mug back on the counter. "And then there's tar."

"Is that why I keep spotting you walking out of Main Street Perk?"

"You should try a decent cup once in a while."

Nick shook his head. "I don't do fancy coffee. I'm old-school that way. Now, stop trying to distract me from interrogating you about your prolonged return to Starlight. Will you and Jack survive a few weeks under the same roof?"

"I'll make it work," Finn answered. "My priority is making sure the bank survives."

"You're doing a good thing, Finn." It was strange to hear so much sincerity in his friend's voice. Nick normally kept things in his personal life light and on the sarcastic side. A defense mechanism, and it meant something to Finn to know he'd been deemed worthy of more than some easy banter.

"Why do I feel like I waited too long?" He pressed his thumb and index finger to his forehead.

"If I'd come back a year ago, maybe First Trust wouldn't be in this position."

"And if you hadn't come back, maybe Jack would have lost everything."

"I know my dad loves to wax poetic about respecting the bank's historical significance in town, but it's still difficult for me to believe he thought he could make it through this crisis without some enormous changes."

"It sounds like he had other priorities."

"He swears he's been given the all clear but I can't help but wonder if he'd even share with me if he was still sick."

"Kaitlin would tell you."

"The keeper of all when it comes to Jack Samuelson."

"I don't know her well," Nick said, draining his mug with a loud slurp. "But I like her. She's friendly without being pushy and seems genuinely dedicated to your dad and the bank."

"I guess." Why was it so hard to admit that he'd been wrong about her? Their time in Seattle had been the most fun he'd had in ages. Not the morning, of course. The meeting with Roger had left him close to shattered at the understanding of truly how much it would take to fix the mess at First Trust. Somehow Kaitlin had sensed it and managed to shore up his tattered emotions with an afternoon at the pop-up amusement park, something Finn had never considered doing in his adult life.

"The town needs the bank, Finn. It's a local institution. So many families and small businesses rely on the support they get there."

He sighed. "No pressure."

"It's an unbelievable amount of pressure. I can't think of anyone better equipped to handle it than you."

"This is not how I imagined adulthood when we were younger."

Nick chuckled. "It was going to be fast cars and no one telling you to clean up after yourself."

"Exactly," Finn agreed, his chest aching for the naive kids they'd been. "Now I'm cleaning up after my dad and you're the one giving tickets to the speeding drivers."

"And I can tell you the exact number of tickets my department has issued over the past five years."

Finn shook his head. "We're pathetic."

"You're rolling out the plan today at the bank, right?"

"Yep."

"Text me later and let me know how it goes. I'm on duty until seven but if you need someone to buy you a beer later…"

"Thanks."

Finn left his friend's house and headed toward downtown Starlight. The sun glinted through the canopy of pine trees as he drove the familiar mountain roads. This valley was still relatively sleepy, even with a steady stream of summer tourists and city dwellers looking to escape to nature for a few days. Growing up, he hadn't appreciated the quiet the way he could now.

He parked next to his dad's Lexus SUV in the parking lot behind the bank, reminding himself that he was here to help. He had no idea how his plan would be received by anyone at the bank, but that didn't make him less committed to carrying it out. There was no other way to turn the ship around.

"I've called a staff meeting for ten," his father announced as Finn entered his office. "Kaitlin tells me I'm not allowed to fight you on any of the silly newfangled stuff you've come up with. I have to *support* you." The words came out almost as a growl, and Finn wasn't sure whether to smile or grimace.

He glanced over his shoulder as Kaitlin walked in behind him, carrying two cups of coffee, and cleared her throat.

"I appreciate what you're doing to help the bank," his father said quietly. "To help me."

"Coffee?" Kaitlin asked, handing Finn a cup.

She didn't make eye contact, which irritated him on some visceral level.

But he focused on his father. Even if Kaitlin had put him up to agreeing, the fact that his father was willing to meant something. He'd talked to his dad the morning after his meeting with Roger, and although Jack had been reluctant to admit how dire the situation truly was, he'd eventually agreed to let Finn implement a new strategic plan for First Trust. It had taken him a couple of days to iron out the details. Now all he needed to do was wrap his mind around the idea of working with his father again.

"I'd like to go over some of the *newfangled stuff*," he said, taking a sip from the cup as he stepped forward. He almost groaned in pleasure at how much better it was than the swill at Nick's. He hadn't stopped at the coffee shop, so he needed the jolt of caffeine in a bad way. "The key is going to be to roll it out quickly."

"I don't like change," Jack grumbled. "Do you know I've eaten the same thing for breakfast every day for the past four decades?"

"Yogurt, granola and half a banana." Finn nodded. "I know. But this isn't like a meal preference, Dad. It's progress."

His father scoffed.

Finn pointed to a device sitting on the desk. "You use a cell phone."

"He likes to text," Kaitlin added.

"I don't *like* to text," Jack grumbled. "It's convenient."

Finn hid a smile as Kaitlin rolled her eyes. "So are some of the changes I'm proposing," he told his father.

"Our customers want to come into the bank, either here or the branch out near the high school."

"Not everyone likes to do their banking on-site these days."

"People are disconnected in the real world. Everything's about apps and social media."

"You can't ignore it." Finn placed his coffee cup on the edge of the desk and pulled a laptop out of his briefcase.

"I'm not ignoring anything."

Except the fact that you're running the family business into the ground, Finn wanted to argue.

"We're going to have a Facebook page," Kaitlin said brightly, clearly doing her best to ignore the tension between the two men. "You love Facebook, Jack."

It was Finn's turn to scoff.

His father's bushy eyebrows drew down over his familiar blue eyes. "I enjoy the quizzes," he said as if that explained everything.

Kaitlin gave Finn a pointed look.

Right. He was supposed to be placating his father so that he'd lend his support to the changes Finn wanted to implement. Antagonizing him would do no good, but old habits and all that.

"I'll friend you," he offered.

"You do that." His father moved a few things from the middle of the desk to make room for Finn's computer. It was a tiny gesture but Finn knew it meant something significant. This desk represented his father's power, and he was making room for Finn.

Finn swallowed against the emotion rising in his throat. Would it have made a difference in how he'd felt about First Trust if his father had made him feel more welcome here when he was younger? Even though it had been clear his dad expected him to take his place at the bank, it had been just as evident that Jack would never relinquish any sort of real power.

Or had that been just an excuse—a rationale Finn had told himself so that he wouldn't feel guilty for walking away from the family business?

"I have a question for you before we get started," his dad said, steepling his hands, elbows on the desk.

"What's that?" Finn lowered himself into one of the chairs positioned in front of the desk. He wanted Kaitlin to take a seat next to him, but she remained standing just behind his father's left shoulder. Finn didn't like it. It made him feel like they were on opposite sides and he wanted—needed—her in his corner.

She hadn't given him a reason to doubt her, despite some of his less-than-chivalrous behavior toward her. She'd made herself scarce since that kiss on the Ferris wheel, but he knew she wanted the best for him, his father and First Trust. Although that should make him happy, he wished her loyalty was only to him. The shadow of the bank had loomed large over every part of his life. It had been his dad's greatest love, often at the expense of his wife and children. No wonder Finn hadn't wanted to dedicate himself to the institution that he'd so often resented during his childhood.

Although here he was, taking an inconvenient absence from his own life to do just that.

"Who's going to manage all of these new initiatives when you trot back to Seattle?"

Finn felt his eyes narrow at the derision in his father's tone. As if he'd be deserting First Trust for something frivolous.

"The staff will handle it," he said, hating the gnawing tightness in his voice.

"Most of them aren't equipped to handle the sort of programs you want to implement."

"They can be trained," Finn insisted. So much for his father supporting what he was trying to do here. He glanced at Kaitlin to see if she realized what was happening. Jack might give lip service to accepting the change, but Finn realized his doubts about his dad had been well-founded, as usual.

Jack leaned forward and pinned Finn with his assessing stare. "Who's going to train them?"

"I will," Kaitlin offered as she came around the desk.

She took the seat next to Finn, just as he'd hoped she would. And as he'd hoped, her presence instantly calmed him. This woman was like his own personal aromatherapy diffuser.

"You don't know anything about marketing at a bank," his father told her, his tone considerably gentler than the one he'd used with Finn.

"Finn will show me." She nodded. "Train the trainer. I've been up late the past couple of nights researching the strategies that other community banks our size have started and the ones that have seen success. I've made some calls to institutions within the region." She held up one hand as she ticked off a list. "There are a few in Washington and a couple others in Oregon. I've scheduled an appointment with the marketing director at Willamette Community Bank. It's only a three-hour drive."

Finn glanced at his dad and found Jack's mouth hanging open much the way he figured his own might be. A moment later, Jack snapped it shut, returning his gaze to Finn. "Did you know about all that?"

"I...um..."

"It was his idea," Kaitlin said without even so much as an eyebrow twitch. "Finn has this under control, Jack. We'll get the staff on board, keep the current customers happy and attract new ones. It's going to work. I know it."

She turned to Finn, and he wasn't sure whether to be buoyed or terrified by the quiet confidence in her dark gaze.

"It's going to work," he repeated. Somehow with Kaitlin in his corner, he believed it.

Kaitlin heard the voices drifting from the break room at the back of the bank's first floor as she walked down the hall.

"I don't know who she thinks she is."

"I've been at the bank for almost twenty years now. Why don't I get to be in charge of this new plan?"

Kaitlin recognized the voices. Liz Martin, the customer service manager, and Cassie Pope, one of First Trust's personal bankers. Both of the women had been kind, if a bit condescending, in the way ladies who considered themselves town mavens could be. But she'd liked them. Cassie had tried to set up Kaitlin with her single nephew. So she was good enough to date a relative but not to take on any real responsibility at the bank?

"She's not even a true local. She shows up in town one day and Jack practically adopts her—"

"As a stand-in since he messed up things with his flesh-and-blood kids, no doubt."

"Do we know who her people are?"

"Does she even *have* people?"

A titter of laughter followed that rhetorical question.

But the casual and crass words weren't funny to Kaitlin. She placed a hand on the wall, needing something to steady herself from the avalanche of emotions pounding through her.

"Don't listen to those two old biddies," a voice said at her shoulder.

She whirled around to find Meg Anderson, one of the young tellers, offering a sympathetic smile. "It's how they deal with change. Those two are like dinosaurs that refuse to see the meteor coming even when fiery rocks start hitting them on the head. Liz is convinced I'm a secret drug addict because of this." She touched the tiny diamond that flashed in her pierced nose.

"I thought they liked me," Kaitlin whispered, somehow unable to pretend the words didn't hurt. More evidence that she'd let herself go soft since she'd come to Starlight. She'd dealt with far worse criticisms than the ones Liz and Cassie were bandying about.

"They do." Meg touched her arm. "I'm not sure why it took Mr. Samuelson so long to start implementing changes around here. Or how the old-timers at the bank managed to convince themselves that business was great. I've only been here six months, but I could see we were heading for disaster."

"I'm not sure it's that bad," Kaitlin said, feeling as though she needed to be loyal to Jack.

Meg shrugged. "I want to keep my job. My boyfriend works for the Forest Service outside town, so we're in Starlight for the foreseeable future. I like eating at restaurants too much to be a waitress. I hate waiting tables."

Kaitlin smiled. "Me, too."

"The ladies will get used to you being part of the management team."

"I'm not management," Kaitlin protested immediately.

"You will be if you do a good job with this." She winked. "No pressure."

"Thanks—I think—for the vote of confidence."

Meg gave her an exaggerated thumbs-up, then continued down the hall and disappeared around a corner.

Kaitlin inched closer to the break room.

"I bet she's sleeping with one of them," Liz said.

"Maybe both of them," Cassie added with a whoop of laughter.

"You've been reading too many of those *Fifty Shades* knockoffs," Liz admonished the other woman.

All the confidence Kaitlin felt talking to Meg vanished in an instant. How could they reduce her to some sort of office stereotype that way? She wasn't sure why she expected better from other women, but she did.

She pressed a hand to her stomach. Suddenly the fruit and yogurt she'd put in the staff refrigerator this morning held no appeal. She turned and headed back toward the front of the bank, through the main lobby and out the antique cherry doors without making eye contact with another soul.

If she had, there was no way she'd be able to hide her embarrassment and shame. She crossed Main Street and hurried into the park that made up a full square block in the center of town. The voices of children in the playground situated in one corner filtered through the air, but she turned in the other direction. There were a few quiet corners in the park, despite its year-round popularity.

Her breathing began to return to normal as she walked along a narrow dirt path canopied by sprawling branches of mature oak trees. At the end of the lesser-used path was a weathered park bench. Sometimes Kaitlin brought her lunch to this spot, but today she just sat.

Closing her eyes, she focused on pushing air in and out of her lungs and releasing the negative emotions that plagued her. Meg was right. The women's petty gibes had less to do with Kaitlin than they did with their own insecurities. She didn't have to take it personally. She wondered if this was how Finn felt when Jack expressed doubt about the plan to save the bank.

If two insulting coworkers hurt her, imagine how much worse it would be for Finn with his own father.

She blinked and glanced up as heavy footsteps sounded on the gravel. As if her thoughts had drawn him to her, Finn walked toward her and then sat down on the empty side of the bench.

"I grew up in this town and I don't think I've ever walked down this particular path until today. I never even noticed it."

"The literal path less taken," Kaitlin said, trying to make her voice light. "I'm all about it."

"I like that about you." His voice sounded even deeper than normal in the quiet of the shady clearing.

She hummed an acknowledgment of his words in the back of her throat, not trusting herself to speak.

"This morning went well," he commented.

"Sure." She swallowed back any other response.

He shifted next to her on the bench, turning so he was facing her. Kaitlin kept her gaze straight ahead.

"You rushed out of the bank just now. What's wrong?"

"I'm fine, Finn. Really."

"What's wrong?" he asked again in the same tone, patient and slow as if he had all the time in the world to wait for an answer.

It practically undid her.

"I heard some of the longtime staff talking about me in the break room. It's stupid and not at all your concern. I need a few minutes to myself. Nothing more."

"Tell me about this talking."

She shrugged. "Petty gossip about how I don't deserve to be leading the charge on any of the new initiatives." She flicked her gaze toward him. "About how I'm probably sleeping with you or your dad as job security."

He let out a breath that sounded more like a hiss. "I hope you marched in there and told them—"

"I ran away. Out here."

"Kaitlin."

She hated the soft admonishment in his voice.

"It makes sense that they'd believe the worst of me."

"Why?"

"Why not?" Now she turned to fully face him. "You did."

His full lips thinned into a tight line. "I didn't know you."

"You still don't trust me."

"I do."

She let out a little snort of disbelief.

He reached out and slowly traced the curve of her ear before his hand lowered to the back of her neck. She didn't realize how much tension she held there until Finn's warm fingers began to gently massage it away.

"I want to trust you, and I appreciate everything you've done to help my dad and support me. Turning things around isn't going to be easy, but you've made me believe it's possible."

"It is," she whispered, letting her eyes drift close and trying not to embarrass herself by moaning out loud.

"How do you know?"

"You may have gone off to do your own thing in the world, but you love your dad and this town. You're going to make things right."

"You'll be a big part of that. Don't let what other people think define you."

She breathed out a small chuckle. "That line should be on a poster with some stylized photo of a rock climber gripping the side of a cliff."

"If I'm the guy in that poster, will you hang it above your desk?"

Her smile widened and she opened her eyes. "Only if you're shirtless."

His laughter rang out in the quiet, and a bird seemed to warble in response. "It's a deal."

She shook her head. "That won't make me any more popular with the ladies at the bank."

He inclined his head, his blue eyes dancing. "You could sell copies."

"Good to know you have a healthy sense of yourself."

"Would you like to confirm my 'sense of self'?" he asked, loosening his tie and unbuttoning the top button of his tailored shirt. She couldn't decide whether she liked him better in his business attire or more casual like he'd been on their afternoon in Seattle.

The truth was, she liked him both ways and

could imagine she'd appreciate him even more with no clothes.

"I'll take your word for it," she said even as her body screamed a silent protest.

"Come on," he coaxed, his voice a sexy growl. "Seeing is believing."

"You're trying to distract me from being upset."

"I'm trying to seduce you," he countered and leaned in to kiss her.

Chapter Nine

He hadn't planned on kissing her again. He wasn't even sure why he'd followed her out of the bank. Finn didn't consider himself either intuitive or a guy who was sensitive to other people's moods.

He was a dealmaker. He managed facts, figures and, most important, profit margins. Rarely did emotion play into his work, and he definitely hadn't become the youngest person to be named a regional director by acting on his emotions. Starlight was messing with him, with who he was on a cellular level. As if the fresh air and slower pace of life had seeped into him, recalibrating everything he knew to be true about himself.

Or maybe it was Kaitlin and the strange, visceral connection he felt with her.

He shouldn't have kissed her but could resist her about as much as he could stop himself from breathing.

The urge was almost involuntary.

Except he was choosing this. Choosing her.

As he slanted his mouth over hers, he heard her sigh. Resignation or desire—he couldn't tell which.

Then she threaded her fingers through his hair, her nails gently grazing his scalp. Lightning sparks of desire skipped along his neck and shoulders. As he was coming to expect with Kaitlin, his tension eased.

Another sort of agitation escalated through him as her tongue licked across the seam of his lips. He opened for her, beyond grateful that she deepened the kiss. There were no words for how much he wanted this.

Luckily, he didn't need words to tell her how he felt. He put all of his desire into kissing her, hoping she understood. Based on her reaction, she felt as much as he did.

Until suddenly she pulled away and stood, straightening her pale pink sweater with a sharp tug.

"I should get back." Her voice was shaky, breathless. "No need to give Liz and Cassie another reason to talk about me."

"I didn't mean for that to happen," he felt compelled to tell her.

"I know," she whispered and then hurried away.

What the hell was wrong with him? He rebuttoned his shirt and straightened his tie. Damn Daniel for dying and bringing him back here, he thought, then immediately regretted it. What kind of a selfish jerk had he turned into that he thought the changes in his life could hold a candle to what Brynn's family must be dealing with now?

In truth, Finn had been given a gift. He had a do-over with his father, a way to clean the slate so he could move forward in his own life without guilt.

This morning had been more difficult than he'd imagined. He was used to managing money. His division employed plenty of people, but he felt so much more of a personal responsibility to the people at First Trust, even though they weren't technically his employees. Chances were good that if his father was forced to sell the bank to a national institution, most employees would retain their positions. But there was no guarantee and, even so, it wouldn't be the same.

He retraced his steps down the path, pausing

to watch the children playing on the park's jungle gym. The equipment had been added since Finn left Starlight. He and his friends had largely roamed the town unsupervised from a young age, gangs of skinned-kneed kids riding bikes, climbing trees and building forts in the surrounding woods.

A woman with thick, dark hair falling over her slender shoulders waved to him. Finn's chest lurched. He hadn't seen Brynn since the funeral, and at that time she'd been surrounded by so many friends and family members he hadn't done much but give her a hug and whisper a few perfunctory words of comfort.

He lifted a hand in greeting and walked toward her. They'd been friends in high school, although unlike Nick, Finn had hung out more with Daniel. They'd played football together all four years of high school, which was as much of a bond as any to teenage boys.

"Hey, Brynn," he said as she met him at the edge of the mulched border that surrounded the rubber base of the play area. "How are you?"

She gave a small laugh. "I've had better months."

"Of course," he answered quickly, embarrassed that he'd asked the question. "Sorry." Shouldn't he know she wasn't doing well? She'd buried her husband a week earlier. How could she be? "I'm really sorry."

"Finn, it's fine." She placed a hand on his arm, her smile warm and comforting. It said a lot about Brynn Hale that her instinct was to make him feel better about shoving his foot in his mouth. "I was making a joke." She frowned. "There seems to be some rule about newly widowed women not being allowed to smile or laugh. I haven't gotten to that part in the instruction manual."

Finn felt his jaw go slack. "There's an instruct—" He inclined his head, studying Brynn. "That was another joke."

"You're catching on," she told him with a quick grin.

"I like that you're smiling."

"I have a son to raise." She turned to gaze toward ten-year-old Tyler, who was totally engrossed in shoveling sand in the oversize sandpit. "He has enough grief of his own without having to deal with mine, as well. I want him to know it's okay to still feel happy, even if he misses his daddy."

"He's a handsome kid," Finn said, at a loss for how to bridge the gap of a decade and their different lives.

"He looks like his father." Brynn's voice was soft, almost sad.

"I see you in him. He has your features."

She smiled, and this time it reached her eyes. "Thank you for saying that."

"You're one of the strongest people I know," he said quietly. "For a lot of reasons."

Her smile faded slightly. "You don't have to feel bad for me. Not for any of it. Tyler is my world, and everything that happened with Daniel pales in comparison to the joy my son gives me. I'd do it all again. Every last moment."

"Even the ones where you and Nick stopped being friends?" he couldn't help but ask.

He heard her audible breath and cursed himself once again. "I'm sorry. It's none of my business."

"Nick and I are still friends," she answered after a moment. Tyler looked up then, glancing around until his gaze landed on her. Finn saw the boy's small shoulders relax. Brynn waved and smiled, and the boy went back to digging. "We're just the kind of friends who don't talk much. But if he ever needed anything, I'd be there for him."

"He'd be there for you, too." He bent his knees until he was at eye level with her. "If you need him, all you have to do is—"

"I don't," she said quickly. "I'm fine."

"Brynn."

"Seriously, Finn." She wrapped her arms around herself, knuckles going white as she grasped the opposite elbows. "I *need* to be fine. For Tyler. For myself. So that I don't let anger and bitterness take over. I don't need Nick or anyone. I've got Tyler, and we're going to be fine."

"I know you will." Finn covered one of her hands with his, letting the warmth from his fingers seep into hers, which were unnaturally cold. "There's no doubt in my mind."

"Thank you," she whispered, nodding. A few of the other mothers sent furtive glances their way, and he was impressed at Brynn's ability to ignore the sidelong looks. "What are you still doing in town anyway?"

"Haven't you heard?" He gave her hand one final squeeze before dropping his. "I'm here to save the bank and become a local hero."

A laugh broke from her throat before she clasped a hand over her mouth. "That's the first time I've laughed out loud since the night he died."

"Glad I can be useful in some way."

"You never struck me as the hero type," she admitted sheepishly.

"That makes two of us."

She studied him for a moment, and he resisted the urge to fidget like a recalcitrant schoolboy under her soft gaze. "It's good you've come back," she said finally. "Life is too short to let the past rule your future."

"My father would appreciate hearing that."

"Also…" She leaned in, as if sharing a secret. "Maybe you could encourage Nick to settle down."

It was Finn's turn to stifle a laugh. "I'm not sure that's in the cards for any of us… I mean…" He cleared his throat. "Nick, Parker or me. Plenty of guys we knew back in the day settled down. Your husband was a perfect example."

Brynn lifted a brow. "Daniel married me, but he never settled. I ignored it for far too long because being the good wife was what people expected."

"I'm sorry that he's gone, but I'm also sorry he hurt you. You deserve better, Brynn."

"We deserve what we choose to accept in our lives," she countered. "I'm going to make sure I start living like I believe I'm worth more." She swiped a quick hand across her cheek. Finn hated the tears swimming in her eyes. "My son needs to see his mom that way."

"I agree," Finn told her, again amazed by her quiet strength. What a fool Nick had been back in high school not to recognize what a prize this woman was in his life. They'd all been fools and probably still were.

"Mommy," Tyler called as he ran toward the climbing wall. "Watch me."

Brynn's smile returned, brighter than ever. "I'm watching, sweetie."

"I should get back to the bank," Finn told her when she returned her gaze to him.

"You're not still honoring that stupid pact the three of you made after high school?" Brynn demanded.

"I…um… How do you know about the pact?"

"Daniel told me years ago. I thought it was just drunken silliness, but the fact that none of you have married and you claim that you aren't going to—"

Finn held up a hand. "The pact had nothing to do with marriage. It was about falling in love."

"So you plan to get married without love?" She shook her head. "Not reassuring me, buddy."

"There are reasons to marry that have nothing to do with love."

"Yeah," Brynn said in a quiet laugh. "I have one."

"I'm not talking about an unplanned pregnancy." Finn felt heat rise up the back of his neck, and suddenly he wanted to loosen his tie again. "Sometimes marriage is more of a partnership than a love match."

"Like a business arrangement?" Brynn asked, a delicate brow rising.

"In a manner of speaking."

She cuffed him on the ear so fast he didn't even see her reaching for him.

"Ouch. Jeez, Brynn, what was that about?"

"Maybe I was trying to knock some sense into you. You're a smart guy, or at least that's the rumor. I don't know what prompted the three of you to commit to not falling in love, but you can't still think it's a smart idea."

"It's worked so far."

"I don't believe that, for any of you. Daniel and I got married because I was pregnant, and things were never perfect. But I loved him as best as I could. It's the only way."

"I hope you find happiness on the other side of this loss," Finn told her. "I'm not built for the kind of love you seem to think is so important."

"You're selling yourself short. Nick and Parker, too, if they think the same way."

He shrugged.

"Go back to the bank," she told him, lifting a hand to gently rub the edge of his ear. "But keep your options and your heart open."

He opened his mouth to argue, but she held up a hand.

"You can't say no to a grieving widow."

"Wow. That's intense. Were you like this in high school?"

One side of her mouth curved. "No, but I like me better now."

Finn chuckled. "I do, too."

He walked back to the bank, trying not to think too much about love or expectations or whether or not his life as he'd created it really was working. These weeks in Starlight were a blip on the radar, and when he had things settled at the bank he'd return to his regular life.

Wouldn't he?

"You're the last one here."

Kaitlin glanced at the clock display in the corner of the computer screen, then quickly clicked the mouse to minimize the screen. She'd managed to avoid Finn since that kiss in the park a few days ago. Heat crept up her cheeks at the memory of his mouth on hers.

"Just finishing up some stuff," she said as she stood, placing a hand on the top of the monitor like she needed to guard it from Finn. "It's only seven."

"Haven't you heard about banker's hours?"

"You're still here, too," she pointed out, trying not to fidget as he looked from her to the computer. She didn't want to lie, but heat crept up her cheeks as she thought about explaining why she was working late tonight.

Of course Finn moved closer, curiosity clear in his eyes. "What are you working on?" he asked.

"Stuff," she muttered.

"Is that an official financial term?"

"I'm finished for tonight," she told him, hitting a few buttons to power off the monitor.

"That doesn't answer my question."

"Your dad is out on a date," she said, hoping to distract him from his irritating interest in what she was doing. "With Nanci, who owns the coffee shop."

Finn nodded. "He told me."

When she came around the side of the desk, he edged closer. "It's nothing," she said immediately.

"You're a terrible liar," he countered.

"I thought you were going to trust me."

"I'm curious as to what has you so ruffled. Tell me you're not trolling some online dating site."

"It's a class," she blurted. "For college."

He opened his mouth, shut it again. "College?"

"Community college," she clarified. "I'm working on my associate's degree in business. It's an online program for working adults."

She shrugged and grabbed her purse from the desk, embarrassed at sharing this bit of herself and irritated at her humiliation over trying to better herself. "I have bigger plans. But my grades in high school were pretty dismal, so I'm going this route and then I'll work on my bachelor's. It probably seems stupid to you." Her voice broke because what she meant was "I probably seem stupid" and she was pretty sure he knew it.

"Why would that seem stupid?" he asked, his voice as soft as fluffy cotton.

She started to move past him, but he stepped in front of her. "Kaitlin."

"I don't need a degree to be Jack's secretary or to wait tables or whatever stupid job I'm going to get when I'm finished here. The truth is, your dad felt sorry for me, and I take care of things. It works for now but I'm not fooling myself into thinking I have a real future. I get that doing these classes is probably just a waste of time."

"If you've got it all figured out, then why work so hard?"

She bit down on the inside of her cheek, willing herself not to answer. She didn't want to say the words out loud. They felt too vulnerable, like the finest blown glass that could shatter at any moment. But there was something about this moment and this man that made her unable to stop the confession. "I want more," she whispered, feeling at once both greedy and liberated from trying to hide her desire.

"Then you should have it," he answered without hesitation.

She glanced up at him through her lashes, unable to lift her head but needing to see his reaction. Her breath hitched as she realized those blue depths held admiration, not judgment. *Breathe in and out,* she inwardly counseled herself. The air goes into the lungs, then out again. Breathing might be an involuntary function, but it seemed that Kaitlin's body had forgotten how to manage it.

Clutching her purse to her stomach, she started to turn away, not sure where she was planning to go.

Finn wrapped his hands around her arms, holding her gently enough that she knew without hesitation he'd release her if that was what she wanted.

Instead she stepped into his arms, pressing her cheek against the warmth of his chest. The purse dropped to the ground as she gathered handfuls of his suit jacket between her fingers, squeezing hard. She did *not* want to cry. She wouldn't cry. Not for such a simple kindness.

Something a stranger would offer, but Kaitlin never expected it from Finn. From anyone. Life and the experiences that came with it had taught her to keep her dreams and desires well hidden. They were weaknesses that the people she thought should care about her would exploit for their benefit.

"Nothing I've seen you do has been a waste of time," Finn said into her hair. He stroked the back of her jersey-knit dress, his touch far too comforting.

"I don't know why it bothers me so much," she admitted. "It's not a big deal. Who cares if I get a degree?" She hiccuped, then continued, "I should be content with the life I have, which is more than I ever thought I'd get."

"Stop selling yourself short." The words were quiet but firm. "You came up with some great ideas for modernizing the way First Trust does business. It was amazing. There's no doubt you can handle more responsibility, and if a degree will give you more confidence, that's great."

"No one but Jack knows."

"Why?"

She forced herself to pull away, smoothing a hand over the wrinkled fabric of his suit jacket. "Because of what I heard Liz and Cassie saying about me. I don't want them to think I'm trying to be better than I am."

"Isn't the point of living—to keep working to become better than we are?" He placed a finger under her chin and tipped it up. "You have a place at the bank. Not waiting tables or whatever other job you think is in your future. You're good here."

She could get used to this…having this man in her corner. But she knew it wouldn't last, even if she allowed herself to raze her walls and open to him. "What about when you're gone?"

"Dad will need you more then," he answered without hesitation.

It wasn't what she wanted to hear. In her silly, stupid, vulnerable heart, she wished for him to tell her that she was changing things. That he could see himself in Starlight, making a life with her at his side.

No.

She wouldn't let herself entertain fantasies that could never come true. She hated how easily Finn had slipped past her defenses.

"He will, Kaitlin," Finn said, and she realized she'd spoken the word out loud.

"You're right, of course." She made her voice purposely light. "I don't know why I let those two get in my head. What do I care what they think? Jack is going to need all the help he can get, especially after you're gone." She picked up her purse. "I'll be here for him, Finn. We'll be fine without you."

He pressed a hand to his chest and flashed a lopsided grin. "Ouch. You don't need to suddenly sound so enthusiastic about the prospect."

"I thought that would make you happy."

"I'm not in a hurry," he said with a shrug, matching his strides to hers as they walked out of the bank.

"But you have your life with all your important plans for your career and a wife who will go perfectly with that."

"There's not exactly a plan for a wife. And my life will still be there when I get back." He held open the door for her, then locked it behind them.

"You like it here," she said with a wide grin. "Admit it. You missed this place."

He rolled his eyes, then hitched a thumb toward the far end of the street. "I might have missed the sweet potato fries at The Acorn Diner. Do you have dinner plans?"

Chapter Ten

Kaitlin's stomach picked that moment to let out a rumbling growl. "I do now," she said. "But I'll warn you, I can practically eat my weight in sweet potato fries."

Finn laughed. "I'd like to see that."

They walked along the sidewalk toward the restaurant, several people stopping to say hello or calling out greetings as they passed. She'd gotten used to the friendliness of small-town life, but she felt a different level of belonging with Finn at her side.

"How is it you've been gone ten years and it's like you never left?"

He grinned down at her. "Trust me, it's a blessing and a curse. Tell me about your associate's degree. How far along are you?"

Anxiety tied her stomach in knots. "I'll be finished at the end of this year."

"Have you thought about where you want to go for your undergraduate?"

They'd arrived at the restaurant, which was the perfect mix of cozy charm and contemporary flare. Kaitlin knew the restaurant had been a staple in Starlight for decades but the owners had managed to keep it fresh. Much of the menu changed seasonally and they always offered a fantastic selection of food and drink that highlighted the local area.

The young hostess showed them to a booth in the back. "You ask the question like it's a given that I'll go on to a four-year degree."

"Isn't that the plan?"

"Well, yes…" Kaitlin pressed her lips together to stop from adding a *but* to her response. "Yes," she repeated with more force. "It's the plan. I'd like to stay in Starlight, so I'll look for online undergraduate degree programs, as well."

"Can I start you two off with some drinks?" a waitress asked as she approached the table. "Oh, hey, Finn. I heard you were back in town."

"Hi, Lauren." Finn greeted the pretty blonde

with a strangely tight smile that Kaitlin didn't understand. She didn't know their waitress personally, although the woman seemed friendly enough. Her pale hair was pulled back into a low ponytail, and she wore a black T-shirt with the restaurant's name silk-screened across the front, a denim miniskirt that showed off a great pair of legs encased in patterned tights and stylish but comfortable-looking ankle boots. "I'll have a beer, please. Whatever you have on tap."

"There's a great IPA from a brewery over in Yakima."

"Sure."

"How are things in Seattle?"

"Fine." Finn's troubled gaze collided with Kaitlin's and she wished she could understand what had him so upset. "Would you like a drink?"

"We've got a real nice pinot grigio from Harvest Vineyards down in Oregon," the waitress offered.

"I'm great with water," Kaitlin said. "Did you two go to high school together?"

"Senior prom," Lauren said with a soft laugh. "Finn bought me the biggest corsage. It was like a weird growth hanging off my wrist."

"So you dated?"

"Not really," Finn said quickly.

"Neither of us were looking for anything serious back then," the other woman confirmed. "That changed for me when I met Seth." She smiled at Kaitlin. "He's my husband. Five years next week."

"Congratulations," Kaitlin said.

"I'm sure Seth was a big step-up from me," Finn said with a surprising amount of bite to his tone.

"Just a better fit," Lauren answered, her delicate brows furrowing. "Do you want to hear about today's specials?"

Finn shook his head. "We've decided."

Kaitlin hadn't even opened her menu, but she wasn't going to argue that point at the moment.

Lauren flashed an uncomfortable smile as she nodded. "What can I get for you?"

"I'll have the pork chop and a salad," Finn told her, keeping his gaze on the menu.

"How about you?" the woman asked Kaitlin.

"I'll do a burger, medium well, with sweet potato fries." Kaitlin handed her menu to the waitress once she finished scribbling the order on her small pad of paper. "Thank you so much. Right, Finn?"

"Yeah," he agreed, offering the waitress a sheepish smile. "Thanks, Lauren. It's been a long day."

"I totally understand that," Lauren told him. "Seth had a meeting at the bank this afternoon to get final approval for a loan to expand his welding shop."

Finn traced the condensation on the edge of his water glass with one finger. "You haven't spoken to him yet?"

Lauren shook her head. "I turn off my phone when I get to work, but he's been working on his presentation for weeks."

Finn looked like he wanted the floor to swallow him whole as the waitress smiled at him expectantly. Taking pity on him, Kaitlin got Lauren's attention and inclined her head. "I think the table across the way is trying to get your attention."

Lauren threw a glance over her shoulder. "Oh, right. I've taken too much of your time already. I'll get that order in right away and bring over your beer."

As she walked away, Finn pressed a finger and thumb to the bridge of his nose. "I should change that beer order to a straight shot of whiskey."

"The news her husband got today wasn't good," Kaitlin guessed.

"It was a fine presentation, but the business isn't a smart investment for the bank right now."

"Why?"

His full mouth tightened. "His credit score was off, and I wasn't confident he could meet the annual revenue threshold. I wish I could be like Mark Cuban on *Shark Tank* and give money to whatever business struck my fancy, but that isn't how things work at the bank."

"But banks are there to help people make their dreams come true."

"Banks are in business to make money."

She shrugged. One of the things that she'd first noticed about Jack was his dedication to not only his bank but also the community as a whole. "By helping people make their dreams come true."

"That's a fairy-tale version of a much harsher reality," he told her and she tried to ignore the sharp edge in his voice. She knew his irritation wasn't directed at her. "This isn't *It's a Wonderful Life*."

Why couldn't Finn see the value of giving someone a chance? "But if the business plan was solid, why can't you give him the money? You know Seth. He's a hard worker and has made a success of the welding company. I know you'd be making a great investment in him."

"It's more complicated than that," he said, then sat back and let out a breath when Lauren returned with his beer.

"Can I tell you a secret?" the pretty blonde asked as she slid the glass of amber-colored liquid in front of him.

"Please, no," Finn muttered at the same time Kaitlin said, "Of course."

"Seth and I are expecting." She placed a hand on her flat stomach. "We haven't even shared it with our families yet, but I had to tell someone."

"Congratulations." Kaitlin forced a smile despite the way her heart hurt at the thought of Seth sharing the bad news he'd received with his pregnant wife. "That's amazing." She kicked Finn under the booth.

"You'll be a great mom," Finn said, which seemed to be exactly what Lauren wanted to hear based on the enormous grin she gave him.

"I hope this doesn't affect anything about Seth's loan," she said, her smile suddenly fading. "I don't want you to think he'll be less dedicated to the business. It's the opposite, in fact. He's so excited to have a kind of legacy for our son or daughter."

"Everything will still be fine with the loan," he promised, then pulled his phone out of his pocket. "In fact, there was something I forgot to mention to Seth earlier today."

Kaitlin's breath caught in her throat as he shot her a pained look.

"I don't have his number in my personal contacts, and I'd like to talk to him tonight if I can. Could you put in his number for me?"

"Of course." Lauren took the phone and tapped the screen. "You're sure it's okay?"

"Better than," Finn assured her, sliding out of the booth. "I'm going to step outside for this call. I'll tell Seth you said hi."

"Awesome. Your food should be out shortly." She looked toward Kaitlin as Finn walked away. "You don't want anything besides water?"

"Water is perfect."

Finn still hadn't returned when Lauren brought their food, and Kaitlin wasn't sure whether to be nervous or optimistic at the length of his absence If he'd changed his mind about the loan… Jack usually had the final say in those types of transactions and couldn't imagine the older man denying Seth his loan if Finn supported it.

She picked up a fry and popped it into her mouth, savoring the way the smoky, sweet flavor complemented the crunchy texture.

"You started without me," Finn said, plucking a fry from her plate as he sat down again.

"What did you say to Seth?" she asked, pushing her plate away and leaning over the table.

Finn took his time cutting into his pork chop. He forked up a bite, his eyes drifting closed as he chewed. "The Acorn isn't fancy, but no one makes better comfort food."

He opened his eyes again, giving Kaitlin that half grin/half smirk she'd come to think of as his signature smile. "This is a first for me."

"What?"

"A woman so infatuated that she ignores an order of perfect sweet potato fries for the pleasure of watching me eat."

As his grin widened, Kaitlin picked up a fry

and flung it at him. It hit him square in the nose before dropping onto the table.

"Good aim," he told her.

"Finn." She narrowed her eyes. "Don't make me come over there."

He chuckled. "I'm not sharing my pork, if that's what you're after."

She kicked him again.

"You're like a professional soccer player. I'm going to have bruises." He made a show of looking under the tabletop. "Are you wearing steel-toed flats?"

"Tell me," she urged, beyond curious to know what had kept him away for so long.

He shrugged. "I talked to my dad, then called Seth. There are conditions he'll have to meet and the APR will be a bit higher than normal…"

"But you're giving him the loan?"

"Yeah. I'm going to help push through a Small Business Association–backed loan." He nudged her plate in front of her. "Now, eat before your food gets cold."

"You sound like somebody's mom." She drew in a relieved breath, happy to know he did care even if he had a difficult time admitting it.

"Like my own," he told her. "Ella and I used to mess around all the time at the dinner table. It was just the three of us when Dad would work late. We gave her a ton of trouble."

"I can imagine," Kaitlin murmured and bit into her burger. She wanted to ask him more questions about the loan, the terms and Seth's response, but she was afraid Finn would change his mind again. What if he redialed Seth and took away his dream because Kaitlin showed too much interest? Because she cared too much about what he'd done?

Stupid. She knew that line of thinking was stupid. Her mom had played those kind of emotional mind games when Kaitlin was a kid, taking her to the pound on a Saturday afternoon to choose a dog, then saying no to whichever one Kaitlin liked best. But Finn didn't operate that way. And besides, why would her opinion matter to him in the least?

Maybe he still had some sort of leftover crush on Lauren, an unrequited-love type of thing, and his giving her husband the loan was his way of trying to take care of her. All very Sydney Carton from *A Tale of Two Cities*, which Kaitlin had read for a world literature course she'd taken last semester.

"That burger must be pretty mesmerizing."

She blinked and glanced up, realizing she'd gotten caught up in her jumbled thoughts.

Finn held out a napkin. "Ketchup on your chin."

"Thanks," she mumbled and dabbed at it, feeling color rise to her cheeks. "The burger is good."

"Are you rushing to eat your food before it gets cold? Did I trigger some kind of childhood memory of your mom's dinner rules?"

She barked out a laugh. "My mom never cared when or what I ate. Dry cereal was a dinner staple in our house when she could be bothered to shop for groceries." She shook her head, refusing to let the emotions from her childhood weigh down on her. "I was wondering about Seth's loan."

Finn studied her for a moment, then shrugged. "I'm going to approve the loan against my better judgment," he admitted. "Dad was thrilled. He'd wanted to give the money to him all along. He'd give money to anyone with a great story and a firm handshake. But that's what's caused some of the problems in the first place. There has to be a balance between lending money to people who need it and becoming overleveraged. It's difficult on the community bank to separate the personal from the professional. At least for some people."

"Like your dad?"

He nodded.

"Maybe Seth will really make a go of it and the welding business will be a breakout success. He could become the star of some sort of welding reality television show."

"I hope so." Finn smiled, then took a drink of beer.

"Why did you change your mind?" she couldn't help but ask. "Was it Lauren? The baby?" She rapped the heel of her palm against her forehead. "Of course that was it. The baby. Babies get people every time."

"It was you," he said quietly, and Kaitlin felt her throat go dry.

"Me?" she asked after clearing her throat.

Lauren brought the check at that moment, and Finn pulled out his wallet to pay for their dinner.

"Tell Seth I expect a tour of his new shop when it opens," he told the waitress with a slight smile, and Kaitlin's stomach swooped and dipped as Lauren processed the simple words and what they meant for her small family.

"He's going to make you proud," she promised, her voice trembling slightly. "Thank you, Finn."

He nodded but focused his gaze on the check, seeming almost embarrassed by her gratitude.

"Are you finished?" he asked when Lauren walked away. "I need to get out of here."

"I'm ready." Kaitlin slipped from the booth and led the way out of the diner, waving to Lauren as they left.

Out on the sidewalk again, Finn started back toward the bank and she hurried to match his long strides.

"Finn, slow down. What's wrong?"

She placed a hand on his arm, tugging until he turned to face her. His blue eyes were dark with an emotion she couldn't name, and his whole body appeared fraught with tension. "I don't want people to look at me like I'm some kind of small-town savior. That isn't who I am. I'm here because…" He shook his head like he couldn't put the reason into words.

"Because you care," Kaitlin supplied. "You're a good man and you care."

"No, I'm a corporate banker. I don't save smaller institutions. I engulf them. Mergers and acquisitions—that's my specialty."

"What did you mean when you said I had something to do with giving Seth the loan?"

He lifted a hand to her face, cradling her jaw in his palm as his thumb traced a path across her cheek. "You were so fervent in your belief, and I wanted to see you look at me the way you are now."

"How am I looking at you?"

"Like you want to be kissed."

She breathed out a soft laugh. "I'm not sure that has anything to do with Seth's loan."

"But you aren't denying it?"

Her heart seemed to skip a beat at the mix of hope and vulnerability in his gaze. This man was so strong, so independent and so damn unwilling to admit that he cared. About his father, the bank and the entire town. But she could see beyond the mask he wore to the honorable core of the man he was meant to be.

He wouldn't push her for more than she could give, and that was just one more thing that made her want him. Kaitlin needed to show him that she was not only done denying her desire but more than willing to take a chance on him. On the two of them.

She might not trust her past with men, but she'd changed since coming to Starlight.

She raised up on tiptoe and pressed her mouth to his, the kiss at once a question and an invitation. One he immediately answered by wrapping his arms around her waist and pulling her closer.

It was different than the kiss they'd shared on the Ferris wheel. That had been a distraction, and this was a declaration. Kaitlin had buried the part of herself that craved physical closeness since coming to Starlight. So many of her bad decisions in life had their start with men, much like her mother. She hadn't wanted that in her new life but couldn't ignore the way she wanted Finn. She didn't want to anymore.

"Come home with me," she whispered against his full lips.

She felt him smile against her mouth. "Since I'm staying with my dad now, I'll be going home with you every night."

"You know what I mean."

He lifted his head, his gaze intense on hers. "Are you sure?"

No.

"Yes."

"Enough that you won't have second thoughts on the drive? We're both parked behind the bank."

"I want you," she said, allowing all of her desire to seep into those three little words.

He grabbed her hand and tugged her around the corner toward the parking lot and, after another lingering kiss, she climbed into her car and followed his taillights onto the darkened streets of Starlight.

He'd been right about her having second thoughts on the way back to the house. Second, third and fourth thoughts were more like it. Something about trailing his sleek BMW in her humble compact sedan reminded her of the differences between them. This town might be her home now, but they came from two different worlds, and she wasn't sure how they'd ever bridge that gap.

Desire was one thing. Reality quite another. Finn's reality was the upper echelons of Seattle society. Country clubs and fancy dinners and women who wore the right clothes and could talk about art or fashion or whatever moneyed women discussed.

Her past made her totally unfit for his world. Before leaving Seattle, she'd barely scraped by and had no ambition beyond tracking down the next party. The crowd she ran with was wild at best and oftentimes bordered on criminal in their crazy antics. While Starlight seemed to put them on a level playing field, she knew that would change as soon as he returned to his life in the city.

Her palms were sweaty on the steering wheel as she worked to keep her breathing steady. The town was steeped in shadows, but the golden light shining from the windows of the houses they passed reminded her of what it felt like to belong here. She'd spent most of her life on the outside looking in, wishing for security and warmth and a place to belong. Jack had given that to her—or at least a chance at it—when he'd hired her to work at the bank.

No one was going to take that from her now, and she wouldn't allow lust to make her forget her priorities.

Even if she wanted to with her entire being.

Chapter Eleven

Finn parked in front of his father's sprawling rancher and walked around back toward the guesthouse, passing Kaitlin's small sedan on the way. No need to advertise his plans for the evening when his father returned home. Not that he wanted to keep whatever this was between Kaitlin and him secret. Unless she did.

Hell, he'd agree to just about anything she asked for the chance to kiss her again. To do more than kiss her. He'd never felt anything like the need pounding through him as he thought about Kaitlin.

He picked up the pace until he was practically

jogging across the lawn, then forced himself to slow down. He didn't want to seem desperate, despite the fact he felt exactly that. Fear flickered along his spine at the thought that she'd change her mind.

I want you.

Those three words had made his body grow instantly rigid with desire. He'd dated plenty of women, both casually and a few who'd ended up with more serious intentions. But he'd never wanted anyone the way he did Kaitlin.

He couldn't understand it. She was beautiful with her golden-blond hair and dark eyes framed by long lashes. But it was more. *She* was more. He had a feeling she could become everything to him if he let her. Which he wouldn't, of course. Couldn't. If he let her in all the way, she might see he actually didn't have enough to give.

He slowed his pace even more as he approached the small cottage. Kaitlin stood on the edge of the cobblestone porch. In the dim moonlight, it was difficult to tell whether she was acting as sentry or rolling out the welcome mat.

"Your dad can't know about this," she said, her voice carrying across the quiet night.

Hoop number one. "Okay."

"*No one* can know," she added.

So she did want to keep it a secret. He ignored

the disappointment that speared through him. This was simply hoop number two. "Fine."

"It ends when you leave town."

Hoop number three. "Why?" He couldn't help but ask, even though he understood the logic of it.

"I'm not part of your world in the city, and I'm building a life here. I don't want people to see me as Finn Samuelson's small-town castoff."

He stepped closer, trying to figure out why her rules for their relationship bothered him so much. Normally he was the one checking off boxes to make sure no one got too attached. He wouldn't let Kaitlin get close, so he should be thanking her for taking care of this aspect. It made him look like less of an unfeeling jerk. But that was the crux of the problem. His feelings for her. "Anyone who would think that isn't worth a moment of your time."

One corner of her mouth kicked up, but the almost smile seemed sad to him. "If that's part of your foreplay routine, you're pretty good."

"I'm better than good," he answered without hesitation. "But it's simply the truth."

"We have an expiration date," she insisted, crossing her arms over her chest.

"Like a gallon of milk," he muttered, then nodded. "It ends when I leave Starlight."

What if he stayed?

The question flitted across his chest like the flutter of butterfly wings, and he tamped it down. Of course he'd return to Seattle. That was his home.

He walked forward and climbed the first step, tall enough that they stood eye to eye even with her on the porch. "Anything else?"

A delicate brow rose. "I like the sound of 'better than good,'" she told him.

How could it be less than perfect with this woman?

She affected every cell of his being like she was an energy that flowed through his veins. The power she had without even knowing was at once heady and terrifying.

"I'm glad." He reached for her, twining his arms around her waist and lifting her into his arms. Her legs settled around his hips and all he could think was that there were too many layers of clothing separating them. "Because I'm done talking now."

As their mouths fused together, he maneuvered them through the front door, grateful she'd left it open. He wasn't sure he'd have the mental where-withal to manage something as mundane as a door-knob at the moment. Not when all of his blood had rushed south at the promise in her eyes.

She laughed when he bumped into the back of the sofa. "You need directions?"

"I'll manage," he said and drew her lower lip between his teeth, eliciting a throaty groan from Kaitlin that nearly had him on his knees.

The guesthouse was tiny, and he and Ella had played there as kids, so Finn easily made his way into the only bedroom.

He slowly—reluctantly—lowered her to the thick carpet that covered the wide-plank floor.

"Tell me you didn't sneak your high school girl-friend in here," she said, making a horrified face as he took a back step.

He shook his head. "Not one," he assured her. "I wasn't that smart."

She gave a small nod, then started on the but-tons of her burgundy-colored dress, the deep color a perfect complement to her dark eyes.

His mouth went dry as inch after gorgeous inch of pale skin was revealed to him.

She began to shrug out of it, then paused, clutching the fabric to her. "You can't just stand there and watch."

He tapped a finger against his chin, as if con-sidering her comment. "I'm having so much fun."

"That isn't how it works." She shook her head. "Not for me."

There was something in her gaze he didn't understand, a kind of vulnerability he hadn't ex-pected from her.

"Tell me what you want."

She bit her lip as her gaze wandered along the front of him. "You aren't wearing your suit jacket."

"It's in the car."

Still holding the fabric of her dress closed with one hand, she pointed at him with the other. "Your shirt and tie." She drew in a breath and added, "Please."

"The *please* is nice." He grinned. "I didn't know being polite could feel like foreplay."

"Before you get ahead of yourself with a bunch of 'nice girl' fantasies, don't go there. I'm going to disabuse you of the notion that I'm fit to star in any of them."

He drew the silk from around his neck and tossed it at her feet. "I'm game for any type of fantasy that involves you."

Pink tinged her cheeks as he unbuttoned his dress shirt, starting with the cuffs, then working his way down the front. The way she watched him was such a turn-on, he was half-tempted to rip the damn shirt apart and get on with things.

But he kept his movements measured, wanting to savor every moment. After yanking the shirt from his waistband, he finished with the buttons and pulled it off, dropping it to the floor.

Her brown eyes widened, and Finn was suddenly grateful for atrocious sleep habits that had him waking before five every morning. He'd made working out a regular part of his routine, not realizing all that sweat and fitness had been solely done so he could impress this woman.

"Your turn," he said, waggling his brows.

She waved a finger up and down in his direction. "I don't look like that."

"What a relief."

She rolled her eyes but loosened her hold on the dress, peeling it away from her body to reveal a lacy skin-colored bra and polka-dot panties.

"Damn," he muttered. "You're so beautiful."

She opened her mouth, then snapped it shut again as she tossed the dress onto a nearby chair. "I hate it when women can't take a compliment," she told him.

"Me, too." He took a step closer. "Especially since I plan to give you plenty of them." Her body was perfection, curvy in all the right places with smooth skin and a smattering of freckles along her chest and belly. He planned to kiss every one.

"I think I could spend the entire night looking at you and I'd be happier tomorrow morning than I have been in ages."

"That's kind of a waste of this bed," she said, hitching a thumb behind her.

"Ah, yes. The bed." He nodded as he moved toward her. "Wouldn't want it to go to waste."

She held up a hand, palm toward him. "Lose the pants."

"No *please* this time?" he asked as he slipped out of his shoes and undid his leather belt.

"I told you I wasn't a nice girl," she said. "You'll have to earn the next one."

"With pleasure," he said, pulling his wallet from a back pocket. He tossed it onto the nightstand before pushing his slacks over his hips and taking the boxers he wore with them for good measure.

He shucked off his socks and then straightened. "Now, who's wearing too many clothes?"

She swallowed audibly as her gaze traveled up the length of him. "I should turn off the light," she said quickly, reaching for the lamp on the nightstand.

"Leave it." He caught her wrist in his hand. "Please."

"*Please* really is quite a sexy word," she said with a small laugh. "But I don't really do this—" she gestured to the bed with her free hand "—with the lights on."

"Feels like the first time," he sang, tugging her to him.

She giggled. "I've definitely never laughed this much."

"I like how bright your eyes are when you laugh," he told her, then nipped at the corner of her mouth. "I like everything about you other than the fact that you aren't naked right now."

She hummed low in her throat as he trailed kisses along her jawline. "Let's do something about that then. Please."

It only took Finn a second to flick open the clasp of her bra. He lowered the straps from her shoulders and leaned back to look down at her as the thin piece of fabric fell to the floor.

His muttered curse was somehow the best compliment she'd ever heard, and her whole body went limp with liquid desire as he covered one puckered nipple with his mouth. He lowered her to the bed, yanking down the comforter and sheet as he did.

She couldn't help but arch into him as he continued his attention to her sensitive breasts. Heat built low in her body, like she was a slow-burning ember ready to explode into flames. Which was exactly what happened when Finn moved his attention lower, peeling her simple panties from her hips and down her legs. He opened her legs, all the while murmuring words of praise about her beauty and all the things he wanted to do to her.

He made her want to offer him every part of her.

Then he stopped talking as she felt his hot breath on her center, followed almost immediately by the gentle touch of his mouth. Not that she was about to admit it—or could even form the words at the moment—but Kaitlin had never allowed a man that kind of access to her body. It felt too vulnerable, and Kaitlin didn't do vulnerability. Not with her heart or her body.

Except now she knew what she'd been missing. Or maybe she hadn't because she couldn't imagine that anyone except Finn could make her feel this way. He'd taken her tamped embers and stoked them into bright, sparking flames. His tongue skimmed along her core and she almost bucked off the bed. It was like nothing she'd ever experienced and she didn't want it to end but felt like she might combust from the intensity of the pleasure tumbling through her entire being.

And when he whispered for her to let go, she had no choice but to obey, her body exploding into a million glimmering flashes all around her. It was as if light and fire rained down over them, consuming her even as it set her ablaze her from the inside out.

"More," she whispered as she returned to herself, because still it wasn't enough. "I want all of you, Finn."

She couldn't let him stop now because if she allowed reality back she was afraid she wouldn't be able to deny what a mistake this was. Yes, she'd been the one to put limits on what was between them but he'd effectively busted through every internal defense she'd created. She was teetering on the edge of fully losing her heart, and still she didn't want it to end.

"Nothing I want more," he said as he reached for his wallet.

She swallowed back a whimper of protest when he shifted away from her, but after sheathing himself with the condom, he returned. The weight of him felt glorious and she tried to remind herself that this feeling of security was an illusion. In a few weeks, his plan for retooling the bank would be in place, and he'd return to Seattle. She'd stay in Starlight and though only an hour separated them, their time together would be at an end.

That was how she wanted it.

Why was it so difficult to hold on to that thought?

"You okay?" Finn asked, his voice so gentle, tears pricked the back of her eyes. She could feel him at her center, but he didn't move, and she knew he would stop this here if that was what she wanted. He was allowing her to choose, willingly giving her the power to decide what happened next. Kaitlin had spent her life being forced into decisions based on fear or anxiety or a host of other unhealthy emotions.

This moment was hers.

She rolled her hips, bringing him closer. "I'm better than okay," she promised. "Please, Finn. Now."

He licked a path from the base of her throat up to her jaw. "You with the *please*," he said, then claimed her mouth.

A moment later he entered her, all heat and velvet strength. Kaitlin moaned, the feel of the two of them joined in this way so right. She knew she'd never be the same but welcomed the change. It was a reclaiming of sorts—of trusting herself to decide without an overarching fear of what would come next.

She wanted to be done with worry ruling her life, and Finn felt like a perfect way to forge a new path. Sensation bathed her in golden light, and she welcomed it. Welcomed everything she hadn't allowed herself to feel.

So what if it ended? This was her moment and as they found their release together, she knew that this moment was all that mattered.

Chapter Twelve

Finn blinked awake early the next morning, a slow grin spreading across his face at the sight of Kaitlin sleeping next to him. Her blond hair spread across the pillow like a slumbering wave. Last night had been…

Amazing. Mind-blowing. Scary as hell.

The last thought had him tensing, and he forced himself to relax again when she stirred with a soft humph. She turned her head but didn't seem to wake, a tiny gift for which he was eternally grateful.

He needed a minute to gather himself and his chaotic emotions. Mostly because the emotions were a shock.

In the throes of passion, it had been easy to rationalize them as a reaction to great sex. Mind-blowing sex. Even this morning, if he really wanted to pretend, he could allow himself to believe that the vague twinge in his chest was the waning afterglow.

But that was a lie.

His heart had shifted sometime in the night, or maybe the overarching pleasure of being with Kaitlin had finally shaken loose the emotions he'd been trying to control. She meant something to him. She made him feel things he hadn't allowed himself to in years.

Which gave her the power to wreck him.

After his mom died, it had been easy for Finn to close down his heart. What other choice did a motherless son have? His father had been too consumed by his own grief to shepherd Finn or Ella through theirs. Finn understood he was stunted by the loss but until now it hadn't mattered.

He'd made himself a success, which was important. More significantly, his two best friends had agreed that the complications of love weren't worth the trouble. He wasn't alone. He belonged to a trio of hard-hearted men, and although it might not be healthy, it worked for all of them.

In fact, he figured the walls he'd built around his heart were a benefit in the long run. When he left Starlight, he hadn't planned to ever marry, but when it became clear it was expected in the firm, he knew he'd be able to choose a wife based on practical criteria. Someone who could be a partner for him. His imagined wife would complement him and he'd support and make her happy to the best of his ability. He simply wouldn't fall in love.

Easy enough.

Only not with a woman like Kaitlin. Last night was proof that he had no defense she couldn't breach, no way to keep any part of himself from her. Or to keep himself from craving all of her.

That simply wouldn't work.

He quietly got out of the bed and gathered his clothes, carrying them out of the bedroom and into the main part of the house.

As he dressed, he tried a million different ways to convince himself he was overreacting. Maybe this was the proverbial sowing of his oats. After all, Kaitlin had made it crystal clear that she didn't want a future with him.

He thought her argument about coming from two different worlds a bunch of nonsense, but it might be the thing to keep them both safe.

Still, he needed time. Distance. A bit of perspective. He wasn't an inexperienced kid reading too much into a night of passion. He would have laughed at his rambling thoughts if they didn't make him feel so damn pathetic.

He started a pot of coffee and then left the guesthouse, lifting his head to the gray sky overhead. A fine mist hovered in the morning air, giving the property an odd, somber quality. A perfect match for his mood.

He let himself into his dad's rancher through the laundry room, remembering all the times he and his buddies had stopped up the utility sink with dirt or gravel they'd gathered from the woods that bordered the backyard for terraria or other boyhood projects. His house had been their central hangout, and looking back on things with the perspective of adulthood, he realized his father had done the best he could. He might not have been emotionally available, but Jack had allowed Finn and Ella to make messes and forts with friends, trashing the house and yard as long as it kept them busy and seemingly happy.

Not that any of them had found much happiness once they were without Finn's mom. He took the stairs two at a time and changed into a T-shirt and shorts before returning to the main floor. It wasn't even six in the morning, so he had time for a run before showering and getting ready for work. He hoped pounding the pavement, or at least the trail that wound through the forest, would help clear his head.

"Late night?" a voice asked as he entered the kitchen.

His father sat in one of the swivel chairs at the island, a newspaper open in front of him. He reminded Finn of some of the older partners at the regional office of his bank, who started every day with a cup of coffee and the *Wall Street Journal*, the same way they had for decades upon decades.

Back in the day, Finn's mom had been the one to gather the morning paper once his father left for work, shoving it into the recycling bin, muttering about how she was a glorified maid.

"Do you miss her?" Finn blurted, then felt color rise to his cheeks when his father's eyes widened.

"It's been almost twenty years," Jack answered, slowly folding the paper.

His plan for a run forgotten, Finn hurried toward the coffeepot next to the sink, both because he needed the caffeine and to give himself an excuse to avoid eye contact with his dad.

They hadn't discussed his mother in over a decade.

"I know," he said as he poured a cup. "But nothing has changed in this house since the day she died. Being back here makes me think of her more, so I can't imagine it's different for you."

"*I've* changed," Jack answered. "I don't need to get rid of frames or tchotchkes that belonged to her. I still regret how badly you and your sister were hurt by her death and how I handled it, but I could never regret the time we had with her."

"Tell me you're not lying about being in remission," Finn whispered.

As if sensing that Finn was on the precipice of losing it, his father stood. "It's the truth, son. I'm not going anywhere. It's good to have you back in Starlight. The bank is going to be okay with your help. I can't tell you how grateful I am that—"

"Wait." Finn held up a hand, a sick pit opening in his gut as instinct flared. "Did you purposely put First Trust in this position so I'd be forced to step in?"

His dad's gaze softened even further. "I haven't been able to force you to do anything since you were in elementary school, and barely even then. I love this town and the people who live here. I think I lost track of the fact that I have to balance running a business with my desire to help people who need it."

Finn studied his father, trying to decide if this was the truth or a master manipulation.

"Come on," his dad insisted. "I couldn't have predicted you'd be back here for Daniel's funeral or that Doug would talk to you about the current state of the bank."

"But I would have heard about it sooner rather than later anyway. You know part of what my division does is liquidating struggling financial institutions."

"The bank has been part of my life forever." His dad shook his head. "I wouldn't sabotage it."

"Fine," Finn answered, but part of him wasn't convinced. "I'm going for a run before I shower. I have a meeting with senior management at eight thirty."

"I'll see you at the office," his dad said as Finn turned for the door. "What made you change your mind about Seth's loan?"

Finn paused. "Nothing in particular," he lied as an image of Kaitlin's dark eyes flashed in his mind. He rubbed at his chest. "The more I thought about it, the more sense it made."

"I'm not sure I believe you," Jack said, "but I'm glad for it."

"Yeah," Finn agreed, not meeting his father's gaze. He wasn't sure when Jack Samuelson had gotten so damn insightful, but he didn't like it one bit.

"One more thing, son," his father called when Finn was almost to the hall. He stopped but didn't turn.

"Kaitlin is special, and not just to me. She deserves to be happy."

At that, Finn turned. "Are you implying that I can't make her happy?"

"Not at all." His father ran a fingertip over the empty ring finger on his left hand. "I'm warning you to leave her alone unless you *plan* to make her happy."

Finn wanted to argue. He hadn't liked being told what to do when he'd been a kid, and he sure as hell didn't now. But he only gave a sharp nod and headed out of the house. Kaitlin deserved happiness, and if his dad wanted to advocate for her, so be it.

He hit the ground at a pace he hadn't managed since he was on the cross-country team in high school. Maybe the physical punishment would clear his head and his heart.

At least it would hurt enough to help him ignore everything else for a time. That might have to be enough.

Main Street Perk had a line of people almost to the door when Kaitlin walked in the next morning on her way to the office. She'd been so baffled at waking to find no trace of Finn that she'd left her travel mug of coffee on the counter.

She struggled not to feel hurt that in the morning light it was as if their night together hadn't even happened. Had it meant so little to him that he'd been eager to make his escape?

It counted in his favor that he'd made coffee for her before he sneaked out. Sort of. The coffee had been thoughtful, but it didn't change the fact that he'd left without a word or note.

She couldn't let herself read too much into either his tenderness while they were together or the unexpected disappearance this morning. She'd been the one to mandate the rules. For all Finn knew, she didn't want anything more than a fun night of passion with him.

Except it had been so much more than that— at least for her. Thank heavens she'd mandated the rules before they got naked. Those guidelines might be the only thing keeping her heart safe.

A few people left the line, grumbling about the wait, and she moved forward. She should really be at work already but her stomach turned to knots every time she thought of facing Finn.

So much for living in the moment as she had last night. Now that the moment was over, the one that had left her feeling satisfied in a way she hadn't realized was possible, all her doubts came flooding back. Doubts about her worth as a person and whether or not she deserved the happiness she'd found in Starlight. Impostor syndrome reared its nasty head like a venomous snake just waiting to strike.

The line moved again, and she tried to tamp down the anxiety that rose like a wave inside her. Maybe she should go for a cup of herbal tea instead of caffeine.

"Can I help you?"

Kaitlin blinked, realizing that she'd made it to the counter, so wrapped up in her own head she hadn't even registered the passing minutes.

A pretty but harried-looking brunette stood on the other side. She flashed Kaitlin a smile that was just this side of panicked.

Although the woman seemed familiar, Kaitlin was almost positive she'd never seen her in the coffee shop. "I'll have a grande skinny vanilla latte."

The woman stared at her for a moment, then grabbed a cup. "Can you repeat the order, but a little slower this time?" She met Kaitlin's gaze and grimaced. "It's my first day, and I'm not exactly up on the ordering lingo."

"I'll take over." A skinny kid plucked the cup and marker the woman held. "Brynn, you can wipe down tables."

The woman's mouth thinned. "Nanci wanted me taking orders," she protested weakly.

"Not when you keep getting them wrong," the

kid answered with a sneer. "You can come back to the counter after the morning rush."

"Sure," the woman agreed. "James will finish your order."

Kaitlin nodded and offered what she hoped was a reassuring smile.

She watched Brynn Hale walk away, shoulders slumped, as James quickly marked the cup with the shorthand for her order, which wasn't overly complicated as coffee drinks went. Still, she felt a huge wave of empathy for Brynn.

She'd only met the woman personally once or twice, but everyone in town knew the story of Brynn's recently deceased husband, whose body had been found in the wreckage of his truck with his alleged mistress. Brynn now had a son to raise on her own, and she imagined the widow had taken this job as a first step in her new life as a single mother.

She paid for her coffee and, after the barista handed it to her, headed for the door. But at the sight of Brynn swiping at her cheeks as she filled the napkin dispenser on the far counter, Kaitlin detoured toward the woman. "It won't be long until you get the hang of things around here," she said, making a show of taking a napkin like that was her main purpose.

Brynn let out a disbelieving laugh. "I drink

black coffee," she admitted. "I don't seem to know what customers are talking about half the time."

"You'll figure it out." She placed a hand on the woman's sleeve. "New beginnings can be hard."

"Harder than anything I've ever done," Brynn whispered, her gaze trained on Kaitlin's hand.

"I'm sorry about your husband," Kaitlin said, feeling like she needed to offer something in the way of a condolence.

Brynn's mouth tightened, but she nodded. "Thank you." She glanced up at Kaitlin. "You work for Jack Samuelson, right?"

It was Kaitlin's turn to nod. "I'm Kaitlin Carmody."

"Nice to officially meet you, Kaitlin. I'm glad Finn is staying in town to help with things at First Trust."

"It means a lot to his dad. I guess you and Finn were friends in high school?"

"We grew up together," Brynn said, her mouth gentling into a small smile. "We all hung around in the same crowd. It was a huge shock when he left town. Everyone assumed he'd take over the bank."

"I think he wanted to make his own way in the world."

"Yeah." Brynn sighed. "Neither Daniel nor I had that choice. I guess that's part of what made him so dissatisfied with his life. I held him back.

His future was determined with one reckless decision on prom night."

"Would you have left Starlight if you had the chance?"

Brynn's eyes widened for a moment, and Kaitlin immediately regretted the question. "I'm sorry. I don't mean to pry into your personal life. It's just that this community feels perfect to me. It's hard for me to imagine why anyone would want to leave."

"It's pretty great," Brynn agreed. "I don't mind the question. I wouldn't have changed anything because my son is the best thing I never imagined happening in my life. He's worth all of it. Now I just need to figure out how to support the two of us." She placed the box of napkins under the reclaimed-wood sideboard. "The woman who owns this place used to babysit me, so she offered me a job and was willing to be flexible with my hours. If possible, I want to work while Tyler is in school."

"I hope you're able to manage that."

"I might need to find something that I can actually handle. Mara Reed did my training and I thought I was ready, but this morning has been a rude wake-up call."

"Like I said, you'll catch on and be whipping up half-caff soy extra-shot lattes in no time."

Brynn laughed, some of the tension easing from her shoulders. "That sounds more like a rap song than a fancy drink."

"Good luck."

Brynn grimaced. "Thanks."

As Kaitlin started for the front door, Brynn called her name. Kaitlin turned.

"Any chance you'd want to grab a drink tonight?" she asked in a rush of breath. She swallowed and added, "Tyler has Scouts on Thursday evenings. It doesn't have to be this week. If you're too busy…"

"I—"

"I'm sure you already have friends," Brynn continued, the words coming more rapidly now. "You've been here a couple of years. I have friends, of course. Mostly from high school. And family. But…I just thought…"

"Tonight would be great," Kaitlin told her. She reached into her purse and pulled out a scrap of paper, quickly jotting down her cell number. "Let's invite Mara, too. She can give you tips on coffee orders. Text me about the time and your address. I'll pick you up."

"Great," Brynn said, folding the small piece of paper and pocketing it.

"Brynn, will you grab the box of lids in the storage room?" the barista called.

She nodded but continued to smile at Kaitlin. "Thank you for the words of encouragement. I'm not sure I'll ever be able to rattle off a mocha, steamed, double-shot whatever, but I have the first inkling of hope that I'll find my new normal, whatever that ends up looking like."

"You will," Kaitlin promised, then headed for the bank. In truth, she owed Brynn a thank-you, as well. She'd let herself sink into a funk far too quickly this morning.

So what if Finn had taken off? He owed her nothing, and she wasn't going to let herself be some overly sentimental woman who made a night of great sex into more than it was.

By the time she walked through the bank's polished mahogany doors, she'd finished half her coffee, which also helped her confidence. A jolt of caffeine and female bonding were a powerful combination.

She waved to Meg at the teller window, then took the steps to the second-floor offices. She'd built in time to review some of the marketing initiatives before the executive management meeting Finn had called, but thanks to her coffee shop detour, she went straight to the conference room at the end of the hall.

Channing Cooper, the chief finance officer,

pumped a fist in the air as she entered. "You owe me a dollar, Finn," he shouted across the room.

Finn, who was speaking to his father near the head of the table, glanced up at Channing and then toward Kaitlin, his brows furrowing as he took in the coffee cup she carried.

"I told everyone you'd stop at Perk," Channing said as he approached Kaitlin. "Finn thought you'd bring something from home."

"My vote was that you'd get to the office early and make a fresh pot here," Jack called, one side of his mouth kicking up.

"But I was right." Channing tapped a bony finger against the side of her cup. "I know you so well."

"That sounds a little creepy," Martha Paige, the bank's operations and human resources manager, told Channing. "Leave Kaitlin alone."

"I don't mean it like that," Channing insisted. "Everyone knows Kaitlin doesn't have a personal life."

"Inappropriate," Martha said with an eye roll. "Go sit down, Channing."

Channing grumbled but did as he was told. That was another thing Kaitlin liked about life in a small town. Even in a business setting, there was a camaraderie that couldn't be faked. She knew there were plenty of mean people in any community, and those two women who'd derided her in the break room certainly proved that people could be jerks no matter what, but she had a place in Starlight.

"I know he was joking," she assured Martha anyway.

"Yeah," the woman agreed. Then she added under her breath, "He only looks like a creeper."

Kaitlin coughed to cover a laugh. "Is the HR manager allowed to say that?"

"Probably not." Martha shook her head. "Sorry. My toddler is teething so no one in the house is getting any sleep."

"We're ready to start the meeting," Jack announced to the room.

As Kaitlin slid into a chair at the far end of the table, her gaze caught on Finn's. His dropped to the cardboard cup, and he raised a brow.

She gave a small shake of her head, then opened her notebook, trying not to make it obvious how much it affected her to be in the same room as him.

Everything about Finn affected her, but she wasn't going to let him know it. Talking to Brynn had been a great reminder that Kaitlin had succeeded at starting over. She'd reinvented her life in this town, and she wouldn't let anything or anyone jeopardize the happiness she'd found there, no matter how good a particular anyone looked naked.

Chapter Thirteen

Finn bit back a growl of frustration as he watched Kaitlin duck from the conference room as soon as they finished the staff meeting.

He couldn't exactly fault her as he had no doubt she was heading for her desk to start on the new work he'd assigned her as he discussed various projects and initiatives for the staff to implement in the coming weeks.

In a short time they'd made decent progress, and he was impressed by the updates he'd been given, especially Kaitlin's headway on the marketing plan. Not that he'd told her that in front of everyone else.

He didn't want to do anything to attract attention to his feelings for her, although it was difficult to believe people didn't see the sparks flying between them.

Unless those sparks were only one-sided at this point.

Why hadn't he stayed with her this morning or woken her with the kiss he'd been dying to give her?

Could he follow her without being obvious? He wanted to find a way to pull her aside and smooth over whatever damage he'd caused by walking out.

He inwardly cursed himself even as he listened to Channing discuss the new risk assessment metrics Finn had suggested. He had no business with her outside the bedroom. She'd made the rules around what was between them abundantly clear. There was no reason he should want to change that, not after one night.

"Mr. Samuelson?"

He focused his attention on the young woman who'd approached him. "Meg, right?" he asked and she nodded with a small smile. "Call me Finn. What can I do for you?"

She glanced toward his father and Channing, then swallowed. "A man named Peter Henry is here to see you. He was asking a lot of questions about the health of the bank downstairs and I didn't want everyone to get anxious. When I asked him about his business at First Trust, he said he had an appointment with you. He's waiting in your office."

"What the hell, Finn?" his father muttered as a hush fell over the staff who remained in the conference room.

"He's here to go over some things on my accounts out of Seattle," Finn lied, knowing that whatever had brought Peter, the chief operating officer of AmeriNat's West Coast offices, to Starlight couldn't be that simple.

"We're getting things on track," Jack said, more to himself than Finn. "No one is going to swoop in and take over at this point."

"I know, Dad."

But Finn also knew that the bank wasn't on solid footing yet. He hadn't been specific at his office about why he was taking time off, allowing everyone to believe it had something to do with his dad's health.

True and not true.

Lies and not lies.

After last night it felt like the only real thing in his life was Kaitlin, but she didn't belong to him. He couldn't make her his true north because there was no scenario where that would lead to a happy ending.

"Thanks, Meg," he said with as much of a smile as he could muster. "It's not about First Trust," he told his dad.

Jack gave a curt nod. "Stop by my office later."

"I will." Before heading to his office, Finn walked at a normal pace down the hall toward his father's.

Kaitlin sat at her desk in the corner of the reception area, her eyes glued to the computer screen in front of her.

As he approached, she glanced up, her expression schooled even as one feathery brow rose in question. "I heard your boss is here."

"It's not about First Trust," he repeated. In response, her lips thinned. "We need to talk," he said quietly, massaging his hand along the back of his neck.

"The way you left this morning said everything."

"You made the rules," he snapped, then shook his head. "I can't leave Peter waiting. Can we talk later?"

She shrugged noncommittally. "I'll be working on the marketing materials for the booth at the art show. We'll talk about that."

"Kaitlin."

Her jaw tightened.

"Please," he whispered.

"That isn't playing fair," she muttered, eyes blazing.

"I don't—"

"There you are."

He fought back a groan as he turned toward the hallway. Peter Henry, chief operating officer of AmeriNat Bank, walked toward him, looking irritated and impatient.

"Hello, Peter. I wasn't expecting to see you in Starlight."

The older man inclined his head. "And I anticipated you'd be back in Seattle by now. I didn't realize the angle you were working here."

Finn squeezed shut his eyes as he heard Kaitlin's sharp intake of breath. "No angle, but we should talk in my office."

"I'm waiting," Peter agreed.

Finn didn't look at Kaitlin again. He couldn't stand to see the disappointment he knew he'd find in her gaze, even though he didn't deserve it.

"This bank's a hidden gem," Peter said without preamble as Finn followed him to the office at the end of the hall. "If they entertained multiple offers, it could start a bidding war. But I'd like to lock it down for AmeriNat before that happens. They have—"

"It's not for sale," Finn said, moving to stand behind his desk.

"Everything's for sale," Peter argued, his quiet tone laced with steel. "The Pacific division needs a win right now, and if you're the one to pull it off, there would be no question about your bid for the partner title."

"I didn't realize anyone had questions," Finn countered. He waited until Peter lowered himself into one of the winged armchairs before taking a seat in the leather desk chair.

"Nothing's set in stone until the board approves it." Peter rested his elbows on the arms of the chair, pressing his fingers together in a way that reminded Finn of his own father. It would be interesting to see Peter and Jack together. Two old-school bankers whose careers had taken very different trajectories. The thing they had in common was that both men were used to being top dog and neither liked to be challenged.

"This is my family's bank," Finn said, as if Peter didn't already know that. "I'm helping my dad return it to financial health."

Peter waved a dismissive hand. "Community banks are a dinosaur in the industry. We both know that, even if your father doesn't. I don't have to remind you that acquiring them is a big part of what your career is based on."

"You don't," Finn agreed, "although it sounds like you just did."

"AmeriNat wants to continue our expansion throughout the Pacific Northwest. I'm not sure why First Trust hasn't come up as a potential purchase before now. Having a bank charter in this part of the valley would be a huge coup for you, Finn. It would also make your dad and his board very wealthy."

"But he wouldn't have his family bank anymore."

"He might not anyway. We can make sure First Trust retains a decent percentage of the local employees and offers fair severance packages to those they let go."

Nausea rolled through Finn's stomach as the metallic taste of bile filled his mouth. Being back in Starlight had reminded him how important the bank was to this community. Not just for day-to-day operations but also because of the relationships his dad had formed and the lives he'd helped to change.

Finn thought about the deals he'd done over the years, and how the banks he'd bought and sold had been anonymous entities. It was simple to determine a bank's worth on paper. Spreadsheets and financial reports showed the facts and figures, but there was more to valuing a small-town business than what could be shown in black and white.

Anger plunged through his veins, mostly self-directed. He'd ignored the lessons he'd learned watching his father's dedication to the family business for so many years. He'd let his resentment and bitterness shadow everything in his life.

Hell, he'd willingly turned his back on his family legacy in order to make his life about the opposite.

"First Trust isn't for sale."

"Be realistic, Finn." Frustration edged his boss's words. "This bank isn't your dream or your future. I have no doubt you'll turn it around for a period of time, but what happens when you return to Seattle? There's no way to guarantee the kind of lucrative offer we can put together will still be on the table."

"I understand." Finn rolled his shoulders, trying and failing to dispel some of the tension weighing on them. "I made a promise to my father."

"You have a commitment to me and to Ameri-Nat," Peter countered.

"The numbers in my division have been top in the country for the past four years. I've done more than my part for you and for AmeriNat."

Peter looked around the office as if assessing the decor. "Needs updating," he said quietly. "Businesses either keep progressing or they fail. Nothing and no one is irreplaceable."

Finn ignored the implied threat in the words. "I'll be finished here and back in the office within the month. Until then, I'm keeping up with clients remotely. In fact, I have a conference call scheduled with Bay Bank."

"Not necessary," Peter answered immediately. "I'm sending Trent to San Francisco. He leaves tomorrow."

"That's my account."

"Not while you're in Starlight." Peter stood, the conversation effectively ended. "It's a pretty little town but way too quiet for men like you and me. We need the thrill of the chase." Peter smiled, and Finn wondered why he'd never realized how smarmy the older man was under his facade of polish and sophistication. "I saw Chelsea Davidson at the club last weekend. I don't know why you ever broke things off with that woman. She looked good, Finn. Very good."

He'd heard rumors of Peter's wandering eye for years although he'd never seen his boss with a woman other than his over-Botoxed wife. But when Peter spoke of thrills, Finn couldn't help but think he was talking about more than making business deals. Was that what happened when a man chose a wife based on whether she could host a decent party?

"I hope Chelsea's happy, and I'll get the files

over to Trent," Finn said quietly. He wasn't going to win a squabble over a client meeting with his boss, so why even bother?

The thought made him almost laugh. He'd never walked away from a fight in his life, but right now he couldn't muster the energy to care.

"Within the hour," Peter advised, then walked out of the office.

Finn pressed two fingers to his temples, which were practically throbbing with tension. He knew the senior banker's appearance in Starlight would raise all kinds of questions about Finn's intentions and master plan when it came to First Trust.

As much as he wanted people to trust him, he'd done little to earn it. He thought he was on sure footing at AmeriNat, but the fact that Peter would so quickly give away his client showed that there was no loyalty from that quarter. Although Finn was officially on vacation, he'd been working his accounts late at night, between meetings and planning at First Trust or in the early-morning hours.

Contrast that with his father, who'd been through months of secret cancer treatments and had taken his hands off the reins at the bank for so long it was in real jeopardy of failing. As far as Finn knew, every one of his employees still showed him respect and loyalty as if he were some benevolent business owner taking care of each of them personally.

Finn couldn't help but wonder what it would be like to lay his head on the pillow each night knowing he made that kind of difference in the lives of the people he employed.

Kaitlin knocked on the door of Finn's office several hours later, growing concerned when he didn't answer.

"Finn?" She knocked again. "At least grunt so I know your creepy boss didn't take an ax to you while he was here."

The door opened a crack, Finn glaring at her from the other side. "Don't you think you would have heard a struggle?"

"It was a joke," she said.

"I'm not in a mood to be funny."

"Lucky me." She held up a brown paper bag. "I brought you lunch."

His eyes narrowed.

"It's chicken salad," she continued. "From The Hole in the Wall Deli. It opened last year. Sal, the owner, smokes the chickens himself and adds the tiniest bit of curry to the recipe. It will ruin you for all other chicken salad."

"The way last night ruined me?" he said, his

voice low and rumbly and doing dangerous things to her insides.

"I doubt that," she answered, then gave a startled yelp as he hauled her into the office, slamming shut the door behind her.

"I made you coffee this morning," he said, and it sounded like an accusation.

"Right before you sneaked out." She couldn't help the words or the accusation that laced her tone. She'd brought him lunch because she cared, but a part of her hated that she cared.

He took the bag from her and turned for the desk. "I get up early. I didn't want to wake you."

"Liar."

"You seemed downright mad in the meeting this morning, but now you brought lunch. Did something change or do I need to worry about you trying to poison me with the chicken salad?"

She shrugged. "I've had some time to think about it, and I realized you were right not to stay." She'd worked hard to convince her heart of that.

"Because…"

"Last night was physical," she said, crossing her arms over her chest. She watched as he pulled the parchment-paper-wrapped sandwich from the bag. "I set up the guidelines, and you were honoring them."

"But this morning was different?"

"Not exactly," she lied. "I woke up ready for…"

He arched a thick brow. "For…?"

"You know." She could feel a blush rising to her cheeks. She hadn't meant to have this conversation but couldn't stand to think of him holed up alone in his office all day. She had no idea why Finn's boss from Seattle had come to Starlight, but it couldn't be good for anyone.

"I'd like to hear you say it."

She blinked. "For you," she blurted. "I woke up ready for you."

Her embarrassment faded as a slow, sexy smile spread across his face.

"I shouldn't have told you that." She shook her head. "We had one perfect night, and that's enough."

"Nope." He placed the sandwich on the desk, then moved toward her, so close that she could feel the heat radiating from him. But he didn't touch her, and she forced herself not to lean into him. "One night wasn't part of the agreement."

"But it would be the smart thing to do," she told him. He smelled like the perfect combination of soap and cologne. It made her want to press her nose to the crook of his neck and breathe him in. Which would be really weird and probably make her seem more obsessed with him than she already felt.

"I disagree." He leaned in and placed a feather-light kiss at the corner of her mouth.

Kaitlin swallowed back a whimper. She should walk—no, run—out of his office now. She needed to be smart. Prudent.

"I think an affair during my time in Starlight..." He drew his tongue across the seam of her lips "...is the perfect arrangement."

"Mmm..." was all she could manage as a thousand sparks zipped through her body like an electric current across a high wire.

"I'll be satisfied." His words vibrated against her mouth. "You'll be satisfied."

She wanted to protest that she could never be satisfied when she knew things with him were temporary. But no. That was the way it had to be. She'd made a vow to herself when she left Seattle that she'd get her life together before getting involved with a man again. She had too rocky a track record—bad decisions and putting her own needs aside to make someone else happy.

The problem was how happy Finn made her. Not just the physical aspect, either. She liked talking to him and the way he made her laugh. He took her seriously, her input at the bank and her dreams of making something more of her life. It was as if with Finn she could see herself as the woman she wanted to be. All of which made him far too dangerous to let herself get carried away.

She opened her mouth to protest but before she could form one word, he kissed her. Just like that she forgot every one of her objections. She could easily lose herself in Finn. She wouldn't, of course. But for the moment she let herself be carried away.

His mouth was warm and deliciously firm. He kissed her like they had all the time in the world to discover each other. That thought had her pulling away. She stumbled back a step, pressing two fingers to her lips.

"We can't do this here," she told him in a rush of breath. One kiss and she'd lost all good sense.

Finn ran a hand through his hair, and it helped to see his chest rising and falling like he couldn't quite get a hold of himself. At least she wasn't the only one affected.

"Sorry," he said. "I've been wanting to kiss you since I opened my eyes this morning. You're cute when you sleep."

She couldn't help but laugh. "I drool."

He grinned. "Cute."

"Right." She laughed again. "You don't need to take off or hide out in your office from me. I don't bite."

"Tell that to my shoulder." He made a show of rubbing it.

"You need to stop that." She leveled a finger at him. "I can't walk around here with a permanent blush. Everyone will notice."

"Your penchant for using your teeth in the throes of passion—" he crossed a finger over his heart "—is our secret. But know that I don't make morning coffee for everyone."

"I did appreciate the coffee," she admitted as he sat on one corner of the desk and then took a bite of the sandwich. "Although I'm glad I forgot my mug and went to the coffee shop. Brynn Hale is working there now."

Finn swallowed. "Seriously? I didn't know that."

"It was her first day."

"How's she doing?" He shook his head. "I ran into her in the park and we talked, but I haven't reached out to her since then. I'm a jerk."

"I doubt she thinks that." Kaitlin absently straightened a stack of papers on the desk. "She seems a little lost but determined to figure things out. I can't imagine having to start over from that kind of loss, especially when everyone in town knows the details surrounding it."

"You don't think she'll leave Starlight?"

Kaitlin shook her head. "Not with Tyler. She needs the support."

"It's a good town for that," he said, popping the last piece of sandwich into his mouth. "It's also a good town for chicken salad."

"You inhaled that thing." She handed him a napkin.

"I skipped breakfast. Lost my appetite once Peter showed up."

"You really didn't know he was coming?"

"I'm not trying to sell the bank," he said, his voice tight.

"People will talk. I think everyone has been trying to ignore that bank takeovers are what you're known for. They trust your father to take care of them…"

"But not me?"

She shrugged. "No one knows you well enough."

"What do you think?" He wadded up the parchment paper as he stood, shoving it in the carryout bag and tossing the whole thing in the trash can. "You know me pretty well after last night."

Did she know him? She wanted to believe that but had enough experience to understand sex and intimacy weren't necessarily the same thing.

"I trust you," she said quietly and watched him visibly relax. "You need to show your face out there." She pointed toward the door. "Go on with business as usual so people see they have nothing to worry about from AmeriNat."

"Do you mind if I sit in on the meeting with the volunteers from the art festival? I should probably try to prove that I'm taking an interest in the local scene and all that."

Kaitlin's heart stuttered as she watched pink bloom on Finn's angled cheeks. He made a show of clicking his keyboard and focusing his attention on the computer screen while he waited for her answer. But his blasé demeanor didn't fool her. He needed her, and although she could tell herself all day that didn't matter, it did. She wanted to be needed by him and not just at the office if she admitted the whole truth.

"It would be good if you're there. First Trust has a history of supporting the community. You can be part of that."

He nodded and flashed her an almost sheepish smile. "It's a plan, then."

She turned to leave.

"Kaitlin?" His eyes turned gentle when she met his gaze. "Thanks for lunch, and I'm sorry about how I left things this morning. One night with you isn't nearly enough."

"I feel the same way," she said softly.

They both glanced toward the door when a sharp knock sounded.

Kaitlin opened it to find Jack on the other side. "How did things go with Peter?"

Finn shrugged and tried to look nonchalant. Kaitlin didn't buy it and doubted his father did, either. "Fine. He had some questions about a deal I'm working on in Northern California."

"Always the power player," Jack said, a muscle ticking in his jaw. "It must feel like you're stuck in East Dullsville here compared with what you're used to."

"I never said that," Finn protested, his tone cool. Kaitlin wished she could make the two of them admit how much they cared about each other. It was so clear, but every time she thought Finn and Jack were making headway on their relationship, they'd slip into this strange, subtle dance for superiority.

"It seems as though there's plenty you haven't said," Jack countered. "But I'm heading out of town until Sunday morning." His shrewd gaze darted between the two of them. "I trust you can handle things while I'm gone."

"Gone where?" Kaitlin asked. "I thought you wanted to finalize your remarks for the opening of the art show."

He waved a hand. "Put something together. Finn will do the talking on Saturday, so you don't need me."

"Of course we do," she argued.

An emotion she couldn't name flashed in the older man's eyes, but he blinked and it was gone. "I'll be an hour away."

"Do you need a hotel?"

"Already arranged."

"Where are you going?" Finn asked.

Jack's shoulders stiffened. "Seattle. You're not the only one who can handle a big city."

Something passed between the two men, and Kaitlin wanted to shake them both.

"Why?" Finn demanded.

"I'm taking Nanci for a weekend in the city," Jack answered, as if it were the most normal thing in the world.

"You've only been on one date with her," Kaitlin pointed out. "Things are moving kind of quickly, don't you think?"

He chuckled. "At my age, time is a bit more relative. Besides…" He inclined his head and gave her a knowing look. "I'm not sure either of you are in a position to talk to me about moving quickly."

Kaitlin felt her mouth drop open.

"Well played," Finn said from behind her.

It wasn't exactly a surprise that Jack would have figured out what had happened between her and his son last night. But being confronted with his knowledge of it was an entirely different thing. It felt a bit like being called out by a parent. Not that her mom had ever cared much what Kaitlin had been doing with boys.

"I'll see you on Sunday," Jack said, patting her shoulder. He winked. "Have a good night."

Kaitlin glanced at Finn as his father walked away. "That was weird, right?"

"Extremely," he agreed, massaging a hand along the back of his neck. "I'm having flashbacks to high school and I just found out I'll have the house to myself."

"Are you planning a big kegger for all your friends?"

He grinned. "I'm planning on you and me and a bottle of wine."

The whisper of promise in his voice made her stomach dance and spin, and then she remembered her date with Brynn.

"I'm busy tonight," she said, grimacing. "Brynn and I are going for dinner and drinks while her son is at a meeting. My friend Mara was going to come with us, but she already has plans. I think Brynn needs some new friends."

"I'm glad she has you, then," Finn told her without missing a beat. "Just be sure to save room for dessert."

She swallowed hard at the promise in his eyes, anticipation already making her body tingle from head to toe.

Chapter Fourteen

"You won't believe who made me the worst cup of coffee I've ever had this morning."

Finn adjusted his baseball cap as he climbed into Nick's truck later that night. "Brynn Hale." He shut the door and reached for his seat belt. "And I highly doubt it was the worst. I've tried that swill you brew."

Nick's mouth fell open. "How did you know that?"

"Kaitlin mentioned that today was Brynn's first on the job at Main Street Perk."

"Are the two of them friends?" Nick turned onto the road that led into town.

Finn had planned to spend the evening alone, going over the bank's commercial loan portfolio and ideas for restructuring distribution within the branch. But neither task appealed and, more important, he didn't want to seem like he was waiting around for Kaitlin to get back from her girls' night.

Of course he'd checked his watch at least a dozen times once he'd changed from his suit and settled in at the table in his childhood kitchen. With his dad gone, the house felt weirdly empty, like he was rambling around with childhood memories as his only companions.

So he'd called Nick, who'd been on his way home from the station and offered to swing by for Finn before heading to Trophy Room, a longtime favorite bar of locals in Starlight.

"I guess." Finn shrugged. "Kaitlin didn't say much other than they were going to dinner tonight."

"She's probably going to Brynn's house." Nick fiddled with the radio dial. "Brynn is an amazing cook."

"But not that much of a barista?"

Nick cringed. "I hate that she's having to do that. Put herself out there in town when everyone knows the circumstances surrounding Daniel's death and what he was putting her through before that."

"Maybe she wants to get out there again. I feel like a schmuck even bringing this up, but it's not like he meant to crash," Finn felt compelled to point out. "It was an accident."

"He was cheating on her," Nick countered through clenched teeth. "I'm not saying that meant he deserved to die, but he wasn't doing right by her. This affair wasn't the first."

"You know that for sure?"

"I pulled him over a couple of times for speeding. Let's just say he was never alone and Brynn wasn't with him on either night."

"You've got to talk to her, Nick."

His friend's knuckles turned white. "I can't. I wouldn't know what to say."

"She was your best friend."

"Years ago, man. A lifetime."

"That doesn't change things. Look at us."

"It's different because we're guys."

"Sexist much?"

Nick thumped a hand on the steering wheel. "I don't mean it like that. Things changed for Brynn and me. We can't go back. We're different people now."

"I don't know," Finn said quietly, thinking of Kaitlin. She was different than any woman he'd ever known. His feelings for her were certainly unfamiliar territory. If he planned to stay in Starlight or if he thought she'd be willing to come to Seattle, would that change things between them?

"I need a beer to have this conversation." Nick parked around the corner from the pub. They got out and started down the sidewalk. In the approaching twilight, Finn could see a variety of lit beer signs in the window. "Now that I think about it, I'd like a beer and a new topic. Let's talk football or the BTUs on my new gas grill."

Finn grinned. "Do you want to hear about the new speaker system I installed at my condo?"

"In great detail," Nick said. "With a beer in one hand."

"And a chicken wing in the other?"

"Now you're talking." Nick held open the door of the bar for Finn. Music, laughter and the scent of stale liquor drifted out.

"Is it strange going out in town being the police chief?" Finn asked as they approached the antique bar. Trophy Room had been designed to look like an old English pub with dark paneling and brass fixtures. Rows of shelves and a few glass trophy cases lined the far wall, as it was a town tradition for local teams and star athletes to donate their medals and trophies to the bar for display.

Nick waved to several people and offered friendly greetings to a few more. This was a neighborhood hangout in every sense of the phrase.

"Not anymore," Nick said as they slid into two empty seats at the bar. "I'm not exactly partying like a rock star around here, but I like to keep an eye on things."

"Hey, boys." Finn smiled as Tanya Mehall, who'd babysat him and his sister in their younger years, approached. "Welcome home, Finn," she said, multiple diamond stud earrings glinting in the light. "Always a pleasure, Chief."

"I didn't realize you worked here," Finn told her.

She let out a husky belly laugh, and Finn remembered that she used to sneak cigarettes out on the back porch when he and Ella were supposed to be watching television. "I've been behind the bar about five years now." She leaned in, her familiar bleach-blond hair and high ponytail a throwback to his childhood. "I'd take taming this crowd at their rowdiest over you and your spawn-of-the-devil sister any day."

Finn threw back his head and laughed. Tanya was ten years older than him and the only babysitter who hadn't refused to return to their house after one night with Ella and him. "Did Dad end up paying you double or triple the going rate?"

"Triple," she said without hesitation. "I earned every penny. What's our girl up to these days?"

"She's a travel nurse, focusing on pediatrics,"

Finn reported. "She does a lot of work in Africa and South America."

"Is that so? The wild child has settled down?"

"I'm not sure about that," Finn admitted. Between assignments, Ella had managed to visit every continent on the planet, often backpacking with friends she made during her travels. Finn had done a fine job of ignoring the pain from his childhood. Ella was still on the run from hers. His sister had channeled her energy for good as a nurse, but she still wouldn't make a commitment to stay in one location for more than a few months at a time. "But she's managing in her own way."

"Aren't we all?" Tanya asked with a wink. "What can I get the two of you?"

Finn and Nick each ordered a beer, with Nick adding wings and nachos. The drinks came quickly and Tanya promised the food would follow shortly.

As Finn took a long pull, he turned in his chair to survey the crowd. He recognized a number of people, and even more looked vaguely familiar. But there were also a handful of newbies sprinkled in, whether visitors to the area or new residents he couldn't say. The fact that Starlight was growing made him more confident about the chances of turning things around at the bank for the long term. He didn't want to admit how much Peter Henry's dismal prediction had affected him.

"Some things never change," he said quietly, taking a strange sort of comfort in that. The social scene he was a part of in Seattle consisted of trendy brewpubs and high-end restaurants. He'd thought that was what he wanted from his life, but the more time he spent in Starlight, the less sure he became.

"Aww, hell, no," Nick muttered and Finn felt the immediate change in his friend's demeanor.

"What's wrong?" He followed Nick's gaze to the back of the bar, where a cluster of high-top tables were situated around a couple of pool tables and a shuffleboard game.

He didn't see anything out of the ordinary at first. Then a burly man in dark flannel shifted and he caught sight of a tumble of golden-hued hair. Awareness shot through him. He couldn't get a clear view thanks to the group of twenty-something men surrounding the table, but by the look on Nick's face, Finn already knew who occupied the table where his friend was staring.

"Did you do this on purpose?" Nick's voice was sharp.

Finn shook his head. "I told you they were going to dinner. Why would two women pick the Trophy Room for dinner?"

"Wings," Nick answered simply.

Finn glanced at him.

"Brynn loves wings," Nick clarified. "Everyone in Starlight knows this place serves the best."

"Sorry," Finn said on a sigh. "We can leave if you want to. I'll tell Tanya—"

"Look at the men," Nick said. "They're clustering around them like bees in a flower garden."

"They're two grown women." Finn took a long drink of beer and forced his gaze away from where Kaitlin and Brynn sat. "I'm sure they can handle—"

"One of them just touched Kaitlin's hair."

Finn was out of his seat in an instant, slamming his beer to the top of the bar.

"Here's the food, boys," Tanya said, placing two heaping plates in front of them. "Enjoy."

"I've lost my appetite," Finn muttered when the bartender walked away. He messed with the brim of his ball cap. "What the hell are we supposed to do now?"

Nick plucked a chip from the plate of nachos, melted cheese oozing off the side. "Pretend you don't care."

"I don't care. Not like that."

"Liar."

Finn gave a sharp shake of his head and then picked up the plate of nachos along with his beer. "Grab the wings."

"I'm not going over there."

"It's about time you talked to her anyway."

"I can't talk to her in a crowded bar."

"You have to start somewhere."

"This isn't about Brynn and me."

Finn grinned. "I'm making it about you. Easier for me that way."

Nick grumbled a protest but followed as Finn weaved through groups of people toward Kaitlin's table. Her eyes widened when she noticed him, but she smiled.

"Hello, ladies," Finn said, placing the nachos in the center of the table. "We come bearing food."

Brynn's mouth formed a small O as Nick approached.

"Hey." One of their male admirers held up a hand in protest. "We were here first."

Before Finn could answer, Kaitlin turned to the guy, her shoulders squared. "Excuse me? You say that like you staked a flag on the moon."

"You know what I mean," the man said with a smile that wanted to be charming. "We're all hanging out. No room for anyone else."

"You're done here now," Nick said, moving forward. Finn suddenly had a clear picture of the serious lawman his goof-off friend had become.

Two of the guys took the hint and stepped back but the third edged closer to Brynn, holding out his phone. "Put your number in and I'll text you later."

It was a good thing Nick was off duty because

Finn was pretty sure his friend would have found an excuse to arrest the guy otherwise.

"No, thanks," Brynn said simply. If she detected Nick's brewing temper, she ignored it.

"We can keep things casual," the guy said, not giving up.

Nick made a sound suspiciously close to a growl. This time Brynn did notice and gave him a quelling glance.

She turned back to her would-be suitor with a saccharine-sweet smile. "Let me set you straight, friend. I've been a widow for less than a month and am now the proud single parent of a son who I had when I was still in my teens. As fun as casual sounds, I'm not sure I have it in me at this point. You want to take that on?"

The man swallowed, his Adam's apple bobbing, and slowly pocketed the phone. "Um…well… I should probably go. Have a good night, then."

"You, too," Brynn said with a little wave. She turned back toward the table. "I guess there are benefits and drawbacks to meeting new people." She took a wing from the plate Nick still held and dipped it in the ramekin of ranch dressing. "I come with baggage, and most everyone in Starlight knows it."

"Everyone comes with baggage," Kaitlin said reassuringly.

"Tyler isn't baggage," Nick muttered, shoving over the nachos to make room for the wings.

"Would you date a single mother who just lost her husband?" Brynn asked conversationally.

Finn tried not to cringe as he watched his friend squirm under Brynn's steady gaze.

"N-not you, of course," Nick stammered after a moment.

Although Brynn's expression didn't change, something flashed in her eyes that made Finn want to slap Nick upside the head.

"Of course," Brynn repeated softly.

"Who wants a nacho?" Kaitlin asked, her voice bright.

"You know what I mean," Nick insisted, not taking his eyes off Brynn.

"I do."

"Besides, you don't want to date," he continued, only digging himself a deeper hole as far as Finn was concerned. "It's too soon."

"Thank you for that insight," Brynn told him wryly.

"The nachos look so good," Kaitlin offered into the awkward silence that followed.

"They're the best," Finn agreed.

Brynn stood. "I think I need another beer to go with them."

"Are you driving?" Nick asked, earning an eye roll but no other response from Brynn.

"Anyone else?"

"I'm set," Finn said.

"Me, too," Kaitlin agreed. "Want me to go to the bar with you?"

"I've got it," Brynn answered and turned away.

She started toward the bar, then veered off to where the three men had moved.

"She can't be doing what it looks like she's doing," Nick whispered.

But indeed, Brynn Hale, the sweetest and most accommodating girl Finn had ever met, took the phone of her flannel-clad admirer, tapped something into the screen and handed it back to him with a smile for the ages.

"She did," Kaitlin said with a chuckle.

Nick rounded on her. "That's not funny, and it isn't the Brynn I know."

"How well do you know her at this point?" Kaitlin asked.

Nick's green gaze darkened.

"Kaitlin's right," Finn said, laying a hand on his friend's shoulder. "Even if you don't want to hear it. Brynn's been a married woman for a decade. She's a mother. You can't go right back to how things were in high school just because Daniel died."

"I don't want to go back to high school." Nick's tone was razor sharp. "But she needs…" He ran a hand through his hair. "I don't know what she needs, but it's not a random hookup."

"Give her some credit," Kaitlin said gently. "I don't know her well, but nothing that she's said to me so far has indicated that her husband's death or the circumstances of it is going to send her off the rails. She wants to create a good life for her son."

Nick hitched a thumb toward the trio of hipster lumberjacks. "Then what was that about?"

"I think it was a reaction to your reaction," Kaitlin told him, and Finn appreciated her honesty. "Finn told me how close you and Brynn were in high school. She's not that girl anymore. If you want to be her friend now, figure out how to do that with the woman she's become."

"Good advice," Finn said, gratified when Kaitlin shifted slightly closer to him.

"Yeah," Nick agreed, then drained his beer. He put the empty glass on the table. "But I'm not sure I know how." He nodded at Kaitlin. "I'm glad you and Brynn connected."

"Me, too," Kaitlin agreed.

"You mind giving Finn a ride home?" Nick asked. He drew in an unsteady breath. "I'm not great company right now, and I don't want to irritate Brynn any more than I already have."

Kaitlin nodded. "Sure."

"I can come with you," Finn offered.

"Stay," Nick answered. "I'll catch up with you later."

"Nick is like a brother to me, but he was out of line," Finn said when they were alone.

"Are you sure he was the only one?" Kaitlin gave him a look like he was a recalcitrant schoolboy.

"What did I do?"

She rolled her pretty eyes. "You know I can handle myself in a bar, right?"

"Yes," he said slowly. "Although I didn't expect to see you here tonight. When you said the two of you were going out for dinner—"

"Brynn wanted wings."

"That's what Nick guessed. Are you mad that we came over?" He shrugged. "Am I cramping your style?"

She flashed a saucy smile that had his blood heating. "I don't have that kind of style, nor do I want it. I'm glad to see you, Finn."

He released the breath he hadn't realized he was holding.

"If we weren't keeping things between us on the down low, I'd kiss you right now."

He groaned softly. "Killing me here, Kaitlin."

"Is Nick interested in Brynn?" she asked suddenly, and all of that glorious heat disappeared.

He glanced over his shoulder to make sure Brynn was still at the bar. "She's newly widowed," he told her as if she didn't know the story.

"That doesn't answer my question. I know they were friends, and then she and Daniel were married when she got pregnant. Did she leave Nick heartbroken back then?"

He shook his head. "It definitely rocked his world along the lines of 'you don't know what you've got until it's gone.' Who knows what their new normal will end up looking like?"

"Where's Nick?"

He turned as Brynn slid back into her seat. "He had to go." Finn smiled. "It's good to see you out, Brynn."

She glanced at her watch. "Actually, you're about to see me disappear. Tyler's car pool will be dropping him off in about twenty minutes."

Finn realized she'd returned empty-handed. "What about that other beer?"

"I didn't want another beer as much as I wanted to avoid Starlight's finest doing his big brother routine with me. Ever since Daniel's death, Nick looks at me like I'm an abandoned puppy. Helpless and pitiful."

"He doesn't think either of those things about you."

She didn't look convinced but only shrugged. "Thank you for a fun night," she said to Kaitlin. "I hope Mara can join us next time."

The two women hugged and Brynn whispered something that had Kaitlin giggling.

"What?" Finn demanded.

"Nothing," Brynn said, then hugged him. "It's nice to have you back in town, even temporarily."

His gut clenched at that reminder, and he purposely didn't look at Kaitlin until Brynn was gone.

"We've got a lot of nachos to get through," he said, his tone light despite the lead balloon currently occupying his insides.

She shook her head. "I don't think so."

Damn. Was this the part where she came to her senses and cut him loose?

Then she leaned closer. "I don't want to ruin my appetite when you promised me dessert. Remember?"

His hulking doubts about the future morphed into a million specks of dust flitting through him. He grabbed her hand and pulled her through the bar like a raging fire licked at their heels. "Where are you parked?" he demanded, surprised he could make his voice work normally when every inch of him was on edge.

She pointed across the street toward her small sedan and he led her forward. Pulling the key fob from her purse, she unlocked the car. They got in without speaking, and Finn wondered if Kaitlin was as blown away by the potent attraction between them as he was.

Then the car lurched forward and she tossed him a sexy grin. "Sorry," she said in a laugh. "You haven't even done anything yet and already my body's reacting."

"That sounds almost like a challenge," he told her, but she playfully swatted away his hand when he would have rested it on her jeans-clad leg.

"I'd like to get home in one piece."

"Good point," he admitted. "I guess for safety reasons you'll just have to imagine all the ways I want to touch you right now."

She sucked in a breath and glanced at him again. "Just so you know, Finn, I have a vivid imagination."

"That's the best thing I've heard all night."

Chapter Fifteen

Kaitlin wasn't sure how she managed the drive
from downtown to the Samuelson property with
all the wicked thoughts swirling through her mind.

Finn didn't say much, but every few minutes
he'd let out a devious little chuckle like he knew
exactly how worked up his implied promise made
her.

"The main house," he told her as she pulled up
the driveway. "I want you in my bed."

She nodded, ignoring the fact that the guest bed
in his father's house didn't belong to him. Just as
she'd ignored Brynn's comment about Finn being

in Starlight temporarily. Kaitlin had learned from a young age to be a master at compartmentalization. She'd had no idea it would serve her so well in her dating life.

Or not *exactly* dating life. If she had to admit the truth, the back-and-forth between Brynn and Nick had gotten to her. Were she and Finn the definition of *casual*? A convenient scratching of an itch neither of them could ignore?

Except nothing about her feelings was convenient. *Complicated* didn't even start to do it justice.

But like a moth drawn to a shining light in the dark, she seemed to have no self-preservation instinct when it came to this man.

She parked the car in front of the house, and he took her hand as they walked to the porch. His thumb traced tiny circles on the inside of her wrist, sending shockwaves of awareness through her body.

Finn was a man on a mission. As soon as they were through the door, he headed for the hallway that led to the bedrooms. "You and me first," he said, his voice low and rumbly. "Actual dessert later." He laced his fingers with hers. "Does that work for you?"

When he glanced at her, she nodded, not trusting her voice to speak. Anticipation built within her, and the moment they crossed the threshold into the guest bedroom, he turned and drew her close.

The kiss was electric, every part of her lighting up like a night sky on the Fourth of July. They tore at each other, need and desire making their movements frenetic. It was difficult to tell where Kaitlin ended and Finn began, which was exactly how she wanted this moment to go.

So when he pulled away, she fought back a whimper of protest.

"I can't go slow," he told her, his gaze at once fierce and tender.

"Then don't." She toed off her shoes and shimmied out of her jeans. "I don't want to wait, Finn."

It was all the invitation he needed. He reached for her again, and they were a tangle of arms and kisses until both of them were undressed and tumbling into the bed together.

Once the condom was in place, he entered her in one long thrust, the shock and pleasure of being filled so completely taking her breath away. They moved together and it was like nothing she'd ever felt. Finn seemed to inherently know exactly how to touch her to drive her wild. It was as if he understood what she wanted before she even realized it.

When her release came, her body turned electric once more and the intensity of the pleasure made her want this moment to last forever. He followed her over the edge a few seconds later. Kaitlin felt like her heart had transferred to the outside of her body, as if she were wearing every bit of her feelings for this man on her skin. Surely he could sense it, that all of her talk about rules and boundaries had disintegrated into a thousand pieces in the wake of what he did to her.

"You're amazing," Finn whispered, rolling onto his back and taking her with him.

I love you.

She rolled her lips inward, pressing them tight to prevent the words from popping out unbidden. If she said those three words to him now, it would ruin everything.

He climbed out of the bed and padded to the bathroom as she tried to control her breathing.

She'd fallen in love with Finn Samuelson. All her talk about being independent and living her own life had just gone straight to hell. Goals and priorities, and she was completely enamored of a man who wasn't going to stay.

How did this make her any different than her mom? Always falling hard for whatever man she took to her bed, brokenhearted when each of them left her behind until she was finally just broken.

Kaitlin had sworn she wouldn't make those same mistakes. Hell, she'd left her old life behind so that she could have a fresh start.

If only Finn felt the same way she did. If only he would stay in Starlight.

She bit down on the inside of her cheek until she tasted blood.

If only she weren't such a softhearted fool.

He'd given her no reason to believe anything had changed between them. In fact, she couldn't shake the conviction that there was more to his boss showing up in Starlight than he was willing to admit. But the way he made love to her—like she was the most precious thing in his world— gave her hope.

Kaitlin hated hope. Hope led to disappointment.

She climbed out of bed and threw on one of his discarded T-shirts.

"You look good in my clothes," he said with a wink as he exited the bathroom. He'd pulled on boxers and a pair of loose basketball shorts. "Are you ready for dessert?"

"Sure," she said, keeping her smile bright. He led the way to the kitchen and pulled out a carton of mint chocolate-chip ice cream from the freezer.

Kaitlin grabbed two spoons from a drawer as Finn took off the lid. "How do you feel about your dad leaving you in charge of the art show?"

He took a spoon from her and sat at the kitchen table, pushing out the chair next to his for her. "I'm suspicious anytime Jack Samuelson voluntarily relinquishes control, but I have no problem making the opening remarks on Saturday. My mom chaired the committee the first year the Starlight Art Festival took place. She'd just taken up watercolor painting and was so excited to make the town some sort of mecca for regional artists. It was the summer before she died, and First Trust has been the event's main sponsor ever since."

"Finn, wow." Kaitlin paused with the spoon halfway to her mouth. "I didn't realize what a personal connection you had to it." She shook her head. "Your dad probably got sick of me trying to convince him to reconsider the amount he'd pledged to fund it. I was worried about the bank's bottom line but had no idea why it meant so much to him."

"I'm sure he appreciated your concern." Finn used one finger to nudge the spoon toward her mouth. "I understand the disconnect, though. It's the same thing I grappled with on Seth's business loan. Things are much simpler when they're just numbers on a page."

"I guess."

He inclined his head. "Or when you establish the rules for something early on?"

Her cheeks heated at the teasing note to his tone. Here was her chance to tell him she wanted to throw her silly guidelines out the window and go all in with him.

But something stopped her.

Doubt. Fear. The possibility that he would break her heart.

"I have another rule for you," she said instead.

His brows furrowed. "I can't wait to hear it."

She pointed her spoon toward him. "No mining for chips."

He glanced down at the container of ice cream, a slow smile curling his lips. He'd dug around, maybe without even realizing it, for the hunks of chocolate embedded in the ice cream. "But the chips are the best part."

She shook her head, trying to keep her expression neutral. "If you dig them all out, the next person will be left with plain ice cream."

"I want the good stuff now," he said unapologetically. He held up his spoon. "I'll share if you say please."

"Please," she whispered, leaning forward. The chocolate was rich and creamy on her tongue. Then Finn kissed her, and after that she forgot all about ice cream.

Finn gulped down another swig of water as he waited to one side of the grandstand on Saturday morning. He'd told Kaitlin he had no problem making the opening remarks for the art festival, but at that point he hadn't considered how his family's history with the event would affect him.

The festival appeared to have quadrupled in size since Finn had last attended. He could still remember that first year. There had been folding tables and makeshift booths with a handful of local artists selling their creations. His mom had been so proud when the last of her watercolors had sold, and she'd insisted on taking the family out to dinner with her profits.

By that Christmas, she'd been gone.

He'd been angry when his dad had stepped in the following year to sponsor the event, offering enough funding to make it worthwhile for the local art community to keep it going. To Finn, the art show had belonged to his mom and he'd avoided downtown annually on the weekend when it took place until the summer he'd left for college.

Now he was back and it was as if his mother's unintended legacy surrounded him.

"We're thrilled to have you with us this year."

He blinked and nodded, forcing himself to focus on Torrey Daniels, the woman who was chairing the event.

"Thanks," he said, clearing his throat when the word came out sounding like a frog's croak.

"Your dad has been so supportive through the

years of the arts community in Starlight. Any-time we have a new idea, he finds a way to make it happen. There aren't too many people like him in the world, willing to put their money toward what they value in life."

Finn sucked in a breath. All the anger he'd felt toward his father through the years felt like so much water under the bridge right now. Maybe Jack had been gruff and unemotional with Finn and Ella, but Finn could clearly see that his dad's love for his late wife permeated everything he did. He guessed that Torrey was in her midforties, with sandy-brown hair cut into a stylish but easy-to-manage bob. She wore a dress of deep purple, a color he imagined his mother would have loved. She would have appreciated everything about the event. The thought made fresh pain engulf his heart, covering the old ache of missing her like an avalanche of emotion.

"Glad to be here," he said, willing the words to sound less lame than they did.

Torrey flashed an awkward smile. "Okay, then. I'm going to start things off, and then I'll ask you to say a few words before I announce the featured artists for this year."

"What does is it mean to be a featured artist?"

"Those are the artists who were given stipends after last year's show," she told him with a frown.

"It's one of the reasons we've gotten so big. Part of the bank's funding goes toward funding artists in each medium. Attendees vote and your father and his committee make the final decision."

"I didn't know that."

"Over the years, several of the artists who've received funding from First Trust have gone on to break out at both the regional and national levels. Many times all a person needs is someone to believe in them."

Finn felt his mouth go dry. "Tell me about it."

"Your father is truly an amazing man."

"I can see why you think that," Finn said quietly, his senses on overload at the influx of new information to process about Jack Samuelson.

Because of Finn's anger, he'd missed out on so much. Not that he'd misjudged his dad exactly. Jack had admittedly been an awful father after his wife died. But that wasn't the whole of him, the way Finn had always believed.

Torrey checked her watch. "Here we go," she told him with an enthusiastic thumbs-up.

Finn clenched and unclenched his fists as he watched her walk toward the podium. She welcomed the artists and the attendees and then thanked the businesses and community of Starlight for their continued support before inviting Finn to join her onstage.

He registered a polite round of applause, but his focus remained on keeping his composure despite the tumult of sentiment his conversation with Torrey had released inside him. "Thank you." He spoke into the microphone, trying not to wince at the low whine of feedback. "I'll be honest," he continued, glancing out at familiar and new-to-him faces. "It's been years since I attended one of these festivals. Before her death, my mom was an aspiring artist and deeply committed to fostering a thriving art scene in Starlight."

He sucked in a breath at what he'd just revealed. Finn didn't talk about his mother's death, and certainly not in this kind of public forum. Another round of applause sounded and his gaze caught and held on Kaitlin. She stood in the center of the crowd and gave him a small smile and nod, like she was proud of him for sharing that bit of himself.

"But I'm happy to be here now," he told the crowd. "I'm impressed by this community and what my father and First Trust have done to support it. In a few minutes, you're going to be introduced to the artists who were funded through a program at First Trust. My dad doesn't just run a bank here in Starlight. He cares about this town and its future. We're all dedicated and hope that when you think about the kind of service you want from a financial institution, you'll remember that commitment."

He took another breath as the understanding of what he wanted from his future dawned on him. He couldn't look at Kaitlin again; otherwise he might rush off the stage and pull her into his arms. She might have rules, but he was about to break every last one of them. He wanted her. For keeps. "We might not be artists at First Trust, but I hope you'll visit our booth and learn more about some of the programs we're offering to help you meet your life goals, no matter what they might be."

As he backed away from the microphone, he couldn't help but notice the applause was more intense than when he'd taken the stage a few minutes earlier.

"You did great," Torrey whispered, gently squeezing his arm as she moved past him.

Finn shook hands with the artists waiting to be introduced, each one thanking him and offering kind words about his father and the way he'd personally supported them over the previous year. Finn wasn't sure whether to be humbled or irritated at how easily his dad seemed to offer encouragement and backing to everyone in his life except Finn.

He couldn't stand to examine the thought too closely or else he'd have to admit his part in that.

Kaitlin was waiting for him behind the line of booths.

"You did great," she said with a huge smile.

His heart hammered in his throat at everything this woman made him feel. Could he say it now? Blurt out that he loved her and hope for the best?

There was no way she couldn't feel something for him. No way his emotions were one-sided. He just had to convince her to take a chance.

"It helped having a friendly face in the audience." He reached for her but she gave small shake of her head, her smile dimming slightly. "We're in public," she whispered.

"I don't care," he answered. "We need to talk, Kaitlin. There's so much…"

"Finn!" He turned as one of the sound guys waved to him from the back of the stage. "Torrey needs you for pictures with the artists."

Finn cursed under his breath.

"Go," Kaitlin said. "I'll be at the First Trust booth all day. We can talk later."

"I don't want to wait."

"Delayed gratification is good for you," she said with a laugh, then stood on tiptoe to brush a quick kiss across his lips. "There's something to tide you over."

"So sweet. I'll find you," he promised before heading back toward the stage.

Chapter Sixteen

It was late in the afternoon before Kaitlin felt like she had a moment to breathe. The bank's booth had been swamped with people all day. Some had been in the crowd that morning and heard Finn's speech, and word of mouth had made talk of First Trust's dedication to the Starlight community spread like wildfire.

Although many longtime locals already did their banking with the institution, Starlight had grown in the past few years. Many of the newer residents were also new to First Trust. Before the recent social media campaign and marketing initiatives, they hadn't done much to attract additional customers.

Jack had always believed that if he engaged in good business practices, he'd have a successful business. Kaitlin wished she'd spoken up earlier about the red flags she'd noticed in the way things had been handled. At this point, they had a good start on making First Trust healthy again, but there was still a lot of work to be done.

She hated to think of doing it without Finn. Why couldn't he see that he belonged in Starlight? His words this morning had caused goose bumps to break out across her arms and legs. He had a history here but also a future.

He'd looked so happy when he'd walked off the stage, and now she wished she'd run into his arms the way she'd wanted to. If he didn't care about being discreet, what did it matter?

She swallowed against the lump rising in the back of her throat. It mattered because her reputation was on the line. As much as she might think he should be in Starlight, until Finn agreed she couldn't put herself out there.

Rolling her shoulders, she glanced down the grassy pathway between the rows of booths. Finn had stopped by several times, but she'd always been talking to people. She'd taken a lunch break but had found him surrounded by a group of Jack's friends, who seemed to be regaling him with embarrassing anecdotes from his youth.

Frustration skittered along the back of her neck. What had he wanted to talk to her about? She hoped with every fiber of her being that it had nothing to do with him leaving town and heading back to his real life in Seattle.

It was too soon. It would be too soon for the rest of her life.

"I'm going to walk around for a few minutes," she told Meg, who'd arrived at the booth minutes earlier for her shift.

"You can even go for the day if you want," the young teller offered. "I think things are slowing down."

Kaitlin nodded. "Thanks, Meg. I'll be here in the morning."

The younger woman flashed a cheeky grin. "No offense, but you might need to get a life."

"You could be right," Kaitlin agreed with a laugh. She wanted a life, here in Starlight with Finn. She'd shut down her emotions when she left Seattle two years ago because they'd caused her nothing but trouble. Being with Finn didn't make her feel weak or powerless. She could be her best self with him, which gave her the courage to believe she could share that she'd fallen in love.

For once, leading with her heart might turn out well.

A jazz quartet played from the grandstand at the center of the park, and she headed there, hoping she'd run into Finn. Her phone was out of battery, so she couldn't call until she charged it. Groups of people still filed along the path and most of the display booths were filled with potential customers. By all accounts, the festival was a huge success, and not for the first time today she wondered why Jack had willingly missed it.

Suddenly she froze as she heard her name called by a familiar voice.

No.

Not here.

She turned, reluctant to face her past and silently praying she'd heard wrong, but there was no mistake. Robbie Marici, her ex-boyfriend and the biggest regret of her life, stood in front of a booth displaying colorful landscape prints.

"You look good, Kaitlin," he said, one side of his mouth curving into a patronizing smirk. "All fresh and clean. It's working for me."

His eyes on her made her feel dirty, and her flight reflex kicked in hard. Panic pricked its way along the back of her neck as she darted a glance around to make sure no one she knew had seen her with this man.

Not that Robbie stood out as anything but a tall, handsome, casually dressed festival attendee. His dark hair was shorter than it had been when they dated, and a few gray strands flecked the sides. He had a naturally lean build and strong features, but there was no misinterpreting the angry glint in his hazel eyes.

"You can't be here," she said, trying to act like this was a normal conversation. "You don't belong."

"Hey, Pot," he said with a dark chuckle. "Meet Kettle. This town isn't where either of us should be, sweetheart."

She gave a small shake of her head and moved out of the way of a couple with a toddler and another baby in a stroller. "I live here. It's my home."

"Right," he agreed, too readily for her liking. "I've been watching you today at your little bank booth. People like you. They *trust* you."

Kaitlin swallowed against the bile rising in her throat. Robbie had been watching her. "So what?"

"So, we can use that to our advantage."

She stepped closer, hitching her head toward the empty area between two booths. Robbie followed, and she ignored the sweat that rolled between her shoulders. It was quieter in the small space, the sound of her pounding heart filling her ears.

"There's no 'we,'" she told him. "There hasn't been for two years."

He shrugged. "I feel like we never really got closure with the way you ran off."

"Closure," she said with a sniff. "Give me a break. What do you want, Robbie?"

"There are a lot of old folks in this town. I'm sure they rely on their friendly neighborhood banker." He leaned in closer. "And if that banker had access to their accounts…"

"Don't even go there." She held up a hand. "First, I'm not a banker. I work at the bank but not directly with customers or their accounts. Even if I did, there's no way I'd get in on one of your stupid schemes. Forget it."

"Come on," he urged. "This place has so much potential."

It did, Kaitlin agreed, but not in the way Robbie believed. Starlight had the potential to be a true home for her, but suddenly her life here felt tainted. She'd been wild in her younger years and knew she might have been convinced to go along with Robbie if she'd stayed with that low-life crowd from her past.

"Just think about it." He reached out a long finger, trailing it over her jawline and making her want to shudder. "Seriously, Kaitlin, the good-girl thing is hot in a novel kind of way. But it's not really you. You're like the rest of us. You got dealt some crappy cards as a kid and life owes you. We all need to take advantage where we can."

"I'm *earning* my place here," she whispered, willing her voice to remain steady.

"I saw your mom a few weeks ago. She was looking kind of rough. I bet some fresh air from a trip out to the valley would help her feel better."

"Don't go there." Kaitlin fisted her hands at her sides as guilt surged through her. She drove into Seattle every month to mail cash to her mother, but they only spoke a few times a year and Cindi Carmody didn't know where Kaitlin lived. She loved her mother but had finally gotten to a breaking point with Cindi's dysfunction and wouldn't invite that into her life again. She also wouldn't let Robbie bring it to her doorstep.

"Give me a call next week when you've had a chance to sit with things." He smiled and she wanted to throw up. "My number hasn't changed."

She didn't move a muscle as he walked past her, brushing against her side in a way that made her think of a slithering snake.

Two years. That was how much freedom she'd had, believing she'd made a clean break from her past. God, she'd been a fool.

She ducked out from behind the row of booths, hurrying toward the street where she'd parked her car this morning. All her thoughts of finding Finn vanished. He'd know immediately that something was wrong. That everything had changed or, more accurately, that it had gone back to the way it used to be.

Fear threatened to swallow her whole, a familiar desolation. How naive to think she'd overcome it. Instead it had been waiting, suppressed by her attempt at achieving happiness but easily set free after a few obscure threats from her ex. But what if they were more than just threats? If he made good on the things he said, the world she'd created would crumble around her in an instant.

It felt as though the life she'd built in Starlight had been little more than a house of cards, blown apart by one gust of menacing wind.

Where did that leave her? Kaitlin didn't know, but she understood nothing in her life could go back to the way it had been when this day began.

Finn stared out the bay window in the breakfast nook of his dad's house the following morning, hoping to see any trace of movement from the guest cottage. Something was definitely not right, and his stomach twisted at the thought that he'd inadvertently messed up simply by acquiescing to his feelings.

Kaitlin had left the art fair yesterday before he'd had a chance to talk to her. He'd called and texted but other than a few irritatingly baffling smiley face emoji, she hadn't responded. Torrey Daniels had asked him to join the festival committee and the featured artists at a reception, so it had been close to eight by the time he returned home.

He'd knocked on the door of the guesthouse, confused and concerned when Kaitlin had opened it only slightly. Her gaze was guarded and he would have sworn she'd been crying, but she told him she was sick and needed a night alone to rest.

As tempted as he'd been to push his way in—and hopefully through whatever walls she was hastening to erect between them—he'd walked away.

Nothing had changed as far as he could tell. Yes, he'd inwardly admitted he loved her and wanted a future together, but *she* didn't know that. Was he that transparent?

And what did it mean that almost as soon as he'd acknowledged his yearning for that type of commitment, she'd shut him out?

He almost couldn't stand to think of it.

"There are binoculars in my office if you really want a close-up look."

Finn turned to see his dad striding into the kitchen, briefcase in his right hand. "How was Seattle?" he asked, eyeing the leather portfolio as his father lifted it onto the counter.

"Productive," Jack answered. "What's going on with the Peeping Tom routine?"

"I'm bird-watching," Finn said dryly. He wasn't about to open himself to his dad's opinion on his love life. "How was a weekend in the city with your girlfriend productive? Don't tell me it's such a whirlwind romance that you went engagement-ring shopping."

His dad scoffed. "Don't be silly. Nanci and I are old friends who enjoy each other's company. She wanted to meet with a potential new coffee bean supplier for her shop and I…" He lifted his gaze to meet Finn's and something about the emotion Finn saw there had his senses kicking into high alert.

"Why did you go to Seattle, Dad?"

"To meet with Peter Henry."

Finn turned from the window, gripping the back of a kitchen chair. "Tell me you were arranging a tee time."

"I'm not golfing with Peter."

"Dad."

Jack opened the briefcase and pulled out a slim folder. "Obviously it will take time, but he worked up an initial offer for First Trust based on the financials you gave to Roger." He slid the manila file folder across the granite countertop. "If you want to take a look."

"What the hell are you talking about?" Finn felt his knuckles start to ache where they ruthlessly tightened on the back of the chair. "He can't come up with an offer in twenty-four hours. It's the damn weekend."

Jack waved away his concern. "Preliminary numbers, but the wheels are in motion."

Finn shook his head. "You're talking nonsense. From the moment I expressed concern about the bank's stability, you've been telling me you wouldn't sell. I've put my life on hold to bail you out, and now that it seems like the plan might succeed, you go to Peter behind my back to—"

"I didn't go to Peter," Jack interrupted, steel lacing his tone. "You're the one who brought him to Starlight."

"He showed up on his own," Finn insisted. "I sent him away with no hope for a deal."

"Do you really expect me to believe that?"

Finn felt his mouth drop open. "Yes. It's the truth."

Jack drew in a deep breath like he was trying to rein in his temper. "I appreciate the work you've put into the bank these past few weeks. It gives us more bargaining power, which I assume was your intent from the start."

"My intent?" Finn muttered. "Are you joking?"

"I've dedicated my life to First Trust," Jack said slowly. "It's our family's legacy."

"I get that," Finn said through clenched teeth.

"But you've also made it clear that it isn't *your* legacy," Jack continued, and the words were like a punch to the gut for Finn. "I don't fault you for it, but I need to think about the future."

The future was all Finn had been thinking about since yesterday. His future in Starlight, and now it was being taken from him before he'd even had a chance to claim it.

"Don't you think you might have mentioned this to me first?"

"I appreciate all you've done," Jack repeated, "but the bank is still mine. I don't need your permission to make decisions about it."

"You never would have given me a real chance," Finn said, bitterness swamping every other emotion he felt. "That's how it's always been. Why do you think I had to leave and not come back for so many years, Dad?"

"We weren't good enough for you," his dad answered immediately.

Finn barked out a harsh laugh. "Try it the other way around. I was never good enough for you. No matter what I did at the bank or in school, it was never enough."

"I'm not going to apologize for pushing you."

"You pushed me right out of your life," Finn whispered.

Jack opened his mouth, shut it again. After a moment he reached forward and plucked the folder off the counter. "You're here now," he said. "But not once have you given me a reason to believe you want to stay."

Fair enough. Finn could admit that to himself, although not out loud.

"Are you going to stay in Starlight?" his father asked, and Finn couldn't help but notice the older man kept any emotion out of his tone. He posed the question as if he were asking Finn what he fancied for dinner.

"Do you want me to?" The question burst from his lips unbidden, and immediately he wanted to take it back. The words revealed too much vulnerability. Finn felt like he had back in high school, trying but never quite feeling like he'd succeeded at garnering his father's approval.

"I want you to be happy."

Finn sucked in a breath, not quite sure how to process his dad's answer.

Then Jack's gaze moved to a place past his shoulder. "What did you do to her?" he demanded.

Finn turned toward the window to see Kaitlin rolling a large suitcase toward her car. As he watched, she popped the trunk and shoved the luggage inside, her movements frantic like she was in a hurry to get away.

"Nothing." He let out a string of curses as she looked over toward the back of his dad's house. Even from this distance he could see the sadness on her delicate features.

"Does she know about your meeting with Peter?" He glanced at his father. Maybe that was the explanation for her strange behavior yesterday.

"No one knows, although she probably understands your time in Starlight is coming to a quick end. I assume you were clear that your arrangement with her was as temporary as your presence at the bank."

Finn didn't bother to offer a retort. He could deal with his father later. Right now, he had to figure out what was going on with Kaitlin.

By the time he'd crossed the lawn, she was hefting out a cardboard box of possessions.

"What's happening right now?" he demanded as he approached her car.

"I'm leaving." She shoved the box into the back seat and straightened. "When your dad gets back, tell him I'll call him."

"He's in the kitchen."

She drew in a breath at that, squeezing her eyes shut for a moment. "I'd hoped to be gone by the time he returned home."

"Gone where?" He reached for her, but she brushed away his hand like she couldn't stand to be touched by him.

"It doesn't matter." She pulled her keys from the front pocket of her jeans. "You're about to return to Seattle anyway. We had rules."

"Forget the rules," he said, frustration making his voice sharper than he meant it to be.

"I can't," she whispered. "When I ignore the rules, I get hurt."

"I'm not going to hurt you, Kaitlin."

She opened her eyes, and he could almost see the sparks flaring in their dark depths. "You're going back to Seattle."

He wanted to deny it. If she'd said the words to him yesterday, he would have. He would have told her he loved her and he wanted to make a life with her here in Starlight. But the folder his dad had placed on the counter minutes earlier had been like a bomb detonating in the middle of Finn's chest. Every doubt he'd had about himself, every moment of feeling unworthy had exploded within him, the shrapnel lodging so deep he wasn't sure he'd ever recover. His father hadn't even bothered to talk to him.

Jack could say what he wanted, but to Finn it felt like an indictment on his own character. Now Kaitlin was ready to take off without a word. He couldn't help but believe she'd sensed the level of his feelings for her and didn't want that from him.

Rules and leaving. Those felt like flimsy excuses for what she wasn't willing to say out loud. *She didn't want him.*

"Ask me to stay," he whispered, needing to hear the words. Needing some reassurance if he was going to lay himself bare at her feet.

Her eyes filled with tears and she swiped a hand across her cheeks. "I…have to go," she said and climbed into her car before he could argue.

Blood roared in his ears as he watched her drive away, and he was pretty sure the fracturing sound he heard was his heart breaking into pieces.

Chapter Seventeen

Kaitlin sat crossed-legged on the couch in Brynn's cozy family room later that evening. The sweet single mother was next to her, and Mara was perched on the edge of the overstuffed recliner on the other side of the coffee table.

"Why didn't you ask him to stay?" Brynn asked gently.

Kaitlin kept her hands over her face as she shook her head.

"Or tell him you loved him?" Mara added.

"I don't love him," she whispered. "I can't. That would be stupid. I gave up stupid when I moved to Starlight."

When neither of her friends answered, Kaitlin lowered her hands to look at them. She both hated and appreciated the gentle understanding she saw in each of their gazes.

She'd driven away from the Samuelson house with no thought to where she was heading. Certainly not back to Seattle, although she'd have to eventually call Robbie and tell him his little plan wasn't going to work with her gone from the bank.

Then there was Jack. She despised herself for leaving without giving him an explanation. But if she told him about her ex, he'd try to fix it. Maybe that would work, but Kaitlin couldn't stand the possibility of her past tarnishing Jack's opinion of her. Granted, she'd shared a lot with him when he'd first hired her at the bank. She didn't want to ever give him a reason to regret the chance he'd taken on her.

Her rational side understood that most of what Robbie said had been bluster and empty threats. But the part about bringing her mother to Starlight was real and enough to terrify her. Why was it so difficult to start over with a clean slate?

"You're not stupid," Mara said, "but you aren't a liar, either. It's obvious you love him, Kaitlin."

"He's a good man," Brynn added, reaching out to give Kaitlin's leg a gentle pat.

Kaitlin had driven to the edge of town, then pulled over onto the shoulder of the highway and cried for what felt like days. Eventually she'd regained her composure enough to turn the car around and drive to Brynn's.

Her new friend had taken in Kaitlin's tearstained cheeks, then led her into the small midcentury ranch-style house without question. Kaitlin had gone into the guest bedroom, flopped onto the bed and fallen into a deep, dreamless sleep, exhausted from the emotional toll the confrontation with Robbie had taken and devastated by how she'd left things with Finn.

She'd woken to afternoon shadows making their way across the pale yellow walls and walked out to find both Brynn and Mara waiting for her. Brynn had not only called their mutual friend, but also arranged for her boy to sleep over at his grandma's house.

"You seem like you might need a real girls' night," Brynn had told her, and Kaitlin had dissolved into tears once again.

Now she managed a smile for Brynn. "He's a really great guy," she agreed.

"And you love him?" the other woman asked.

Kaitlin managed a shaky nod. "I do."

"Love complicates everything," Mara muttered. "We're better off without it."

"Stop." Brynn held up a hand. "Now you sound like Finn, Nick and our friend Parker. The three of them made some silly pact back in high school to never fall in love."

Kaitlin frowned. "Why?"

"Probably to avoid getting hurt," Mara offered, picking up her wineglass from the coffee table and taking a long drink. "My divorce just about did me in, and think of what happened to Brynn." She tipped her glass toward Kaitlin. "Maybe you've got the right idea."

"I still believe in love," Brynn said. "Finn isn't your dirtbag ex-husband or Daniel. The guys might think they're going to avoid getting hurt, but they'll also miss out on the happiness true love can bring." She smiled at Kaitlin. "You don't want to let that happen."

Kaitlin glanced at Mara, who was staring into the glass of chardonnay like the golden liquid contained the answers to life's greatest mysteries.

"She's right," Mara said after a few moments. "Even though I hate to admit that I was an idiot for choosing the man I did. But you'll be an idiot if you walk away from Finn Samuelson."

"It's too late." Kaitlin sniffed. "I already ruined things by running away. Both Samuelson men probably hate me at this point."

Brynn laughed softly. "I highly doubt that."

"What if I go back and he doesn't want me?"

"You won't know unless you try," Mara said.

"I'll have to tell him about my ex and his threats."

Both women nodded.

"And how bad things really are with my mom." Kaitlin sighed. "I've kept so much of myself and my past hidden."

"Give him a chance," Brynn urged. "It's scary to show someone the ugly parts as well as the pretty, but you won't be able to truly move forward unless you do. And imagine how great it would be to have someone choose to love you no matter what."

"For better or worse," Mara murmured.

"I don't know your ex-husband," Kaitlin told her friend, "but I can guarantee he was the idiot and not you."

Brynn nodded. "You'll just have to pick someone better next time."

"Oh, no." Mara placed her wineglass on the table as she shook her head. "It's all peachy that the two of you still want love, but I'm done with it. The only kind of lovin' I need in my life is battery-operated."

All three women laughed at that, and Kaitlin felt some of the tension ease from her chest. She'd run away out of fear and a bone-deep belief she didn't deserve happiness because her past was less than perfect. But Finn had been the one to tell her that the point of life was to keep working to get better. She'd done that in Starlight, and it was past time she owned the good about herself as well as the rough stuff.

"I need to talk to him," she whispered. "I need him to know I love him and I want a future together if he'll have me."

"He'd be a fool not to," Brynn said. "No one has ever accused Finn Samuelson of being a fool."

"Thank you for everything." Kaitlin shifted on the sofa cushions, leaning over so she could hug Brynn, then smiled at Mara. "I don't know what I would have done today without the two of you. I'm not used to having real friends, and I want you to know how much I appreciate you both."

"Right back at you," Brynn murmured. "It's kind of comforting to know I'm not the only one working to get my life on track. Cry all you want, but don't ask me to make you another convoluted coffee drink."

Kaitlin chuckled at that.

"You know what I like to say?" Mara leaned forward in her chair. "Chicks before di—"

"No!" Brynn and Kaitlin shouted to the other woman at the same time before dissolving into more laughter.

"You're going to meet some kind, gentle man," Kaitlin said, pointing at Mara. "And it's going to change everything."

"Can he be a librarian?" Mara asked dryly. "I bet a librarian would be free of drama."

"Swipe left for no drama," Brynn said. "That's the new dating theme."

Kaitlin uncrossed her legs and stood. "I have to go back to Jack's and find Finn. We need to have this conversation in person." She pressed a hand to her stomach. "Then I'm driving to Seattle to deal with my past instead of running from it."

"That a girl," Mara said, also rising. "I'll walk out with you. Thanks for the wine, Brynn. If we're all going to be messed up, it should be together and with wine."

Kaitlin groaned softly, prompting Mara to reach out and squeeze her hand. "Scratch that," the other woman said. "You're fixing things. Brynn is still hopeful and I'm holding out for a librarian hero."

"With wine," Kaitlin added, returning the gentle squeeze.

"This has been the most fun I've had in ages," Brynn told them as she opened the front door. "Other than the part where you were sad and crying, of course."

"Of course," Kaitlin repeated, giving both of her friends a final hug before walking to her car. Her breath caught at the sight of her possessions crowded in the back seat. Once she saw Finn, she then needed to talk to his dad. Jack had done so much for her since she'd arrived in Starlight, but it was time for her to stand on her own two feet. She wanted her own apartment—maybe she'd even adopt a cat.

Yes, she loved Finn with her whole heart, but she owed it to both of them to move forward, claiming the life she believed she deserved. She'd never thought of herself as particularly strong, but that was who she was going to strive to become. Finn had helped her have confidence in herself and now she had to convince him they were meant to be together.

His car wasn't at Jack's when she pulled up the driveway. She thought about calling him but got out of the sedan instead and walked toward the front door of the rambling rancher.

The door opened as she lifted her hand to knock.

"You took off like a bat out of hell," Jack said, one thick brow arched.

"Can I come in?" she asked.

"Always," he answered immediately, stepping back to allow her to enter. "Did Finn do something to you?"

She followed him into the formal living room, sinking down onto one of the wingback chairs that flanked the upholstered sofa. "My ex-boyfriend came to Starlight yesterday."

"The lowlife from Seattle?" Jack frowned as he lowered himself onto the couch. "The one who caused so much trouble for you?"

She nodded. "I haven't talked to him for over two years, but it felt like no time had passed. He was the same jerk I remembered, only this time he wanted me to help him with a scheme to cheat elderly customers at First Trust out of their savings."

"Bank fraud," Jack muttered, rubbing a hand across his jaw. "He's gotten ambitious in your absence."

"Or more reckless," she countered. "I told him no, but he made some stupid threats."

Jack's shoulders stiffened. He was no longer a strapping young man but could still appear quite formidable when he set his mind to it. "We won't let him hurt you, Kaitlin."

She swallowed at the emotion welling in her at his words. "*I* won't let him hurt me. He also talked about bringing my mom to Starlight, and I don't want that. She's toxic but I got caught up in his anger and the power he used to wield in my life. I felt like the only way to deal with it was for me to leave. You've been so good to me, Jack. I'd never knowingly bring trouble to your doorstep."

He chuckled even as he shook his head. "Girl, I've dealt with my wife's death, cancer and almost losing my family's bank. There's no trouble you can throw at me that I can't handle."

"You shouldn't have to—"

"You're part of this community," Jack reminded her. "We take care of our own around here. But nothing is going to be solved by running away."

"I understand," she said, trying to be discreet as she swiped at the corners of her eyes before the tears started to fall. "Do you know when Finn will be back?" She offered a watery smile. "Turns out I've fallen hard for your son, Jack. I need him to know that."

A trickle of unease crawled across the back of her neck at the look Jack gave her. "I guess you weren't the only one who made some hasty decisions without thinking them through."

"What do you mean?"

His shoulders slumped, and she was suddenly reminded of how frail he'd been after his cancer treatments. He'd regained his strength, but now all that vigor seemed to vanish in an instant. "I started the process of selling the bank to AmeriNat."

Kaitlin felt her mouth drop open. "Jack, you can't do that. Why?"

"Having Peter Henry show up here threw me for a loop. I assumed it was Finn's way of giving me the message that it's time to sell. Besides, I want to start thinking about retirement, and I have to ensure the bank is in good hands before I do that. I've made plenty of mistakes but none bigger than letting my grief drive a wedge between me and my son and daughter. Finn has a huge career and he's done it with no help from me. He helped right things at First Trust but I can't expect him to drop everything he's worked for and take over here in Starlight. I didn't think that was what he wanted anyway."

"You didn't talk to him before meeting with Peter?"

Jack shook his head. "I thought I was right, but now he thinks I did this because I don't want him to run First Trust."

Kaitlin thought about Finn's words as he stood next to her car. *Ask me to stay.*

He'd wanted her to throw him an emotional lifeline, and she'd walked away. He wanted to know his dad believed him, and Jack had made a deal without Finn's knowledge.

Her heart clenched at the thought of how hurt and betrayed he must feel right now.

"He's gone back to Seattle?"

"He packed his bags and took off within an hour of you driving away."

"I'm going to make it right with him," she said,

forcing a confidence in her tone that belied the doubts swirling through her mind.

"Maybe for the two of you," Jack said weakly. "But I've pushed him away too many times."

"It's never too late," she insisted. "We have to believe that. I love Finn with all my heart and I know just as strongly that he belongs in Starlight. I can fix this, Jack."

The older man flashed a tender smile. "If anyone can, I know it's you."

Kaitlin swallowed back her uncertainty and returned Jack's smile. This was her chance to prove she had what it took to claim the life of her dreams. And only her entire heart hung in the balance.

"Let's go over the situation one last time so I'm clear about it. You fell in love with an amazing woman, saved the bank and realized how much our hometown meant to you. But no one actually came out and handed you the future wrapped up with a neat little bow so you put on your best pouty face and walked away?"

Finn glared at Parker Johnson over the rim of his beer bottle. They'd been ensconced in a back booth at the Irish pub around the corner from Finn's building for most of the night. It was after eleven, and the events of the day were catching up with Finn. He stifled a yawn and said, "That's not exactly how I'd describe it."

"Which doesn't change the truth of my summation."

"You realize we're not in court at the moment? It's not actually going to help anyone for you to rake me over the coals."

"No worries." Parker patted his shoulder. "This is just a pro bono service I'm providing for a friend."

"With friends like that…" Finn muttered. He'd called Parker on the drive to Seattle, not wanting to spend the evening on his own recounting the one-two punch his dad and Kaitlin had delivered earlier in the day. Parker had been on his way back from a weekend kayaking trip to the San Juan Islands and had finally met up with Finn at O'Malley's after dinner.

No one had more issues with their father than Parker, and as a divorce attorney, he also saw the worst ends of relationships. Finn figured his friend would be up for a venting session to help Finn transform the bulk of his pain to anger. Anger was way easier to deal with than heartbreak.

Instead, Parker had basically told Finn he was acting like a scared, stupid, immature baby-man, which Finn didn't appreciate in the least. But after a couple of beers and a bit of perspective, Finn had to admit his friend had a point.

"Listen," Parker said, aiming a finger toward Finn like a laser pointer. "If there were guarantees in love, then I'd be out of a job. People take chances and most of them get burned in the fallout when things go bad."

Finn blinked. "Is this a pep talk?"

"I'm getting to that part," Parker promised. "Kaitlin is amazing, but she's had her share of hard knocks. She needs you to step up and show her that you're different. Be the man she needs, Finn."

"What if she doesn't actually want me?" Finn forced himself to voice his greatest fear. "If you remember, this is why we swore off love. No risk of getting hurt."

"No chance of really being happy," Parker shot back before draining his glass of whiskey.

"Right." Finn drew in a long breath. He didn't have to ask about Parker's happiness. They were enough alike that Finn already understood. He'd thought his life was fine. He'd had everything under control and that was how he wanted it. Until Kaitlin had spun his world and his heart around in circles, in the process making him see things in a brand-new way.

He could never go back to how it used to be.

Parker placed his palms flat on the scuffed tabletop and leaned forward. "And in case you haven't already realized it, your dad has always wanted you to have the bank." One side of Parker's mouth lifted. "He had a backward way of showing it, but that doesn't mean it isn't true. The question is what you want your life to be. It's all there but you have to stop messing around and claim it."

Finn huffed out a laugh. "Really? You missed your calling as a therapist, Parker."

"Divorce attorney. Therapist." Parker slapped a hand on the table, then stood. "I have many talents."

"I'm going back," Finn said quietly.

"I know." Parker winked. "You can send a bottle of Glenlivet to my office as thanks for the counseling services. Just be sure you never need my courtroom skills."

Finn nodded. "I'll make her happy if she'll have me."

"Good luck."

They went their separate ways on the sidewalk, and anticipation spiraled through Finn as he thought about how to win Kaitlin and make things right with his dad.

He needed some plan…a grand gesture. He glanced at his watch as he entered his building. It was too late to call or text now. In the morning he could…

He stopped in his tracks as the elevator doors swished open and Kaitlin walked into the empty lobby.

She pressed a hand to her chest as her gaze crashed against his, and he wondered if her heart was pounding in the same way as his.

"Hey," she whispered. "I knocked on your door, but obviously you weren't home."

"You're here." *Nice work, Finn. Master of the obvious.* He closed his eyes for a moment and willed himself to regain control of his tumbling emotions.

She looked so beautiful with her blond hair falling around her shoulders and the slight hint of a blush that colored her cheeks. She wore a simple gray sweatshirt and faded jeans, and Finn immediately gained a new appreciation for cotton as sexy.

"I came to the city to see my ex-boyfriend," she told him, her tone measured.

"Oh." Talk about a kick in the—

"He showed up at the art festival yesterday," she continued. "It was bad, Finn. He was nasty and made threats."

Every protective instinct he had went on high alert. "What kind of threats? If he hurt you I'll—"

"He didn't," she assured him. "I won't let him hurt me again, and I made sure he knew that. But he did make me doubt myself." She paused, took a breath. "I was freaking out. That's why I left your dad's the way I did. I'm sorry. It was a cowardly mistake."

"You're one of the bravest people I know," he told her, moving closer. He wanted to reach for her but stopped short. There was too much to say first. "I'm the coward."

He cleared his throat, needing to find the right words. "I wanted to know you were a sure thing before I told you how I felt. That's how afraid I've been of getting hurt." Unable to resist, he took her hand, lacing their fingers together. The feel of her soft skin against his gave him the courage he needed. Now that he had her again, he'd do anything not to lose her.

Even risk his heart.

"I love you, Kaitlin, with my whole heart. I thought I was protecting myself by keeping people at a distance, but there was no way I could resist you. I don't want to because you make me happier than I ever imagined I could be. So happy that it scares the hell out of me." He lifted her hand and brushed a soft kiss across her knuckles. "I know how much it's going to hurt if you don't want me. But if you give me a chance, I promise I'll spend the rest of our lives trying to be the man you deserve."

She extended a finger against his lips. "I have something I need to say."

He waited, not moving or even daring to breathe.

"I love you, Finn Samuelson." A slow smile

spread across her face. "And I'll always be a sure thing with you."

Relief and joy spreading through him, he pulled her closer. She twined her arms around his neck as he kissed her, his heart finally settling into a place that he knew would be his forever home.

"No more rules," he said against her mouth. "It's you and me, Kaitlin. All in."

"Forever," she promised, then pulled back. "What about Starlight?"

"It's home," he said with a quiet certainty that felt like the most natural thing in the world. "I'll make sure my dad doesn't sell the bank, and we're going to be the most boring small-town couple Starlight has ever seen."

"I'll learn to garden," she said with a laugh.

He grinned. "I'll coach Little League."

She kissed him again. "I don't care what we do as long as we're together."

"Forever," he whispered, finally understanding that true love was always worth the risk.

* * * * *

Don't miss the next book in the
Welcome to Starlight miniseries,
available in September 2020
from Harlequin Special Edition!

And in the meantime, look for
these great small-town romances:

Her Homecoming Wish
by Jo McNally

The Marriage Rescue
by Shirley Jump

The Right Moment
by Heatherly Bell

Available now wherever
Harlequin Special Edition books
and ebooks are sold!

WE HOPE YOU ENJOYED
THIS BOOK FROM

HARLEQUIN
SPECIAL
EDITION

Believe in love. Overcome obstacles. Find happiness.

Relate to finding comfort and strength in the
support of loved ones and enjoy the journey
no matter what life throws your way.

6 NEW BOOKS AVAILABLE EVERY MONTH!

HSEHALO2020

COMING NEXT MONTH FROM

H HARLEQUIN
SPECIAL EDITION

Available March 17, 2020

#2755 FORTUNE'S GREATEST RISK
The Fortunes of Texas: Rambling Rose • by Marie Ferrarella
Contractor Dillon Fortune wasn't always so cautious. But as a teenager, impulse
led to an unexpected pregnancy and a daughter he was never allowed to know.
Now he guards his heart against all advances. If only free-spirited spa manager
Hailey Miller wasn't so hard to resist!

#2756 THE TEXAN TRIES AGAIN
Men of the West • by Stella Bagwell
Taggert O'Brien has had a rough few years, so when he gets an offer for the
position of foreman at Three Rivers Ranch, he packs up and leaves Texas behind
for Arizona. But he was not prepared for the effect Emily-Ann Broadmore—a barista
at the local coffee shop—would have on him or his battered heart. Can he set aside
his pain for a chance at lasting love?

#2757 WYOMING SPECIAL DELIVERY
Dawson Family Ranch • by Melissa Senate
Daisy Dawson has just been left at the altar. But it's her roadside delivery, assisted
by a mysterious guest at her family's ranch, that changes her life. Harrison McCord
believes *he* has a claim to the ranch and is determined to take it—but Daisy and her
newborn baby boy have thrown a wrench in his plans for revenge.

#2758 HER MOTHERHOOD WISH
The Parent Portal • by Tara Taylor Quinn
After attorney Cassie Thompson finds her baby's health is at risk, she reluctantly
contacts the sperm donor—only to find Woodrow Alexander is easily the kindest,
most selfless man she's ever met. He's just a biological component, she keeps
telling herself. He's *not* her child's real father or the husband of her dreams...right?

#2759 DATE OF A LIFETIME
The Taylor Triplets • by Lynne Marshall
It was just one date for philanthropist and single mom Eva DeLongpre's charity.
And a PR opportunity for Mayor Joe Aguirre's reelection. Giving in to their mutual
attraction was just a spontaneous, delicious one-off. But as the election turns ugly,
Joe is forced to declare his intentions for Eva. When the votes are counted, she's
hoping love wins in a landslide.

#2760 SOUTHERN CHARM & SECOND CHANCES
The Savannah Sisters • by Nancy Robards Thompson
Celebrity chef Liam Wright has come to Savannah to rebrand a local restaurant. And
pastry chef Jane Clark couldn't be more appalled! The man who impulsively fired
her from her New York City dream job—and turned her life upside down—is now
on her turf. And if the restaurant is to succeed, Liam needs Jane's help navigating
Savannah's quirky culture...and their feelings for each other.

HSECNM0320

SPECIAL EXCERPT FROM

H HARLEQUIN
SPECIAL EDITION

*Harrison McCord was sure he was the rightful owner
of the Dawson Family Ranch. And delivering Daisy
Dawson's baby on the side of the road was a mere
diversion. Still, when Daisy found out his intentions,
instead of pushing him away, she invited him in, figuring
he'd start to see her in a whole new light. But what if
she started seeing him that way, as well?*

*Read on for a sneak preview of the next
book in Melissa Senate's
Dawson Family Ranch miniseries,*
Wyoming Special Delivery.

Daisy went over to the bassinet and lifted out Tony,
cradling him against her. "Of course. There's lots
more video, but another time. The footage of what the
ranch looked like before Noah started rebuilding to the
day I helped put up the grand reopening banner—it's
amazing."

Harrison wasn't sure he wanted to see any of that. No,
he knew he didn't. This was all too much. "Well, I'll be
in touch about that tour."

*That's it. Keep it nice and impersonal. "Be in touch"
was a sure distance maker.*

She eyed him and lifted her chin. "Oh—I almost
forgot! I have a favor to ask, Harrison."

Gulp. How was he supposed to emotionally distance
himself by doing her a favor?

She smiled that dazzling smile. The one that drew him like nothing else could. "If you're not busy around five o'clock or so, I'd love your help in putting together the rocking cradle my brother Rex ordered for Tony. It arrived yesterday, and I tried to put it together, but it has directions a mile long that I can't make heads or tails of. Don't tell my brother Axel I said this—he's a wizard at GPS, maps and terrain—but give him instructions and he holds the paper upside down."

Ah. This was almost a relief. He'd put together the cradle alone. No chitchat. No old family movies. Just him, a set of instructions and five thousand various pieces of cradle. "I'm actually pretty handy. Sure, I can help you."

"Perfect," she said. "See you at fiveish."

A few minutes later, as he stood on the porch watching her walk back up the path, he had a feeling he was at a serious disadvantage in this deal.

Because the farther away she got, the more he wanted to chase after her and just keep talking. Which sent off serious warning bells. That Harrison might actually more than just like Daisy Dawson already—and it was only day one of the deal.

SPECIAL EXCERPT FROM

HQN

*An inheritance brought her to Magnolia,
but love just might keep her there...*

Read on for a sneak preview of
The Magnolia Sisters,
*the first full-length novel in Michelle Major's
brand-new series!*

"Give me the beach property. It's where I—"

"The terms of the will are clear," Damon interrupted. "Meredith, you inherit the Reed family home. Avery, the gallery and other commercial space he owned downtown. The ranch belongs to Carrie now."

Meredith narrowed her eyes. "Like hell it does."

"Sit down," Damon told the fiery brunette.

"You don't tell me what to do." Meredith's voice cracked on the last word, and she swallowed hard. "I'm out of here. Niall didn't care about me when he was alive. Why should I care about his wishes now that he's gone?"

Before anyone could stop her, Meredith fled the room. The door to the office banged against the wall in her wake.

Damon looked toward Carrie, sympathy and compassion filling his tired gaze. "It's worse than we thought. He owed a lot of money to a lot of people, Carrie."

She gave a shaky nod. "I'll deal with it," she promised. "Give me some time." She rose from her chair and turned to Avery. "I have an appointment right now but will be at the gallery after one. Come by and we'll talk about… next steps."

Then she left, as well. Avery wanted to follow but felt rooted in place. A man she didn't know—her father—had left her his art gallery along with some over-mortgaged real estate. She'd never even seen one of his paintings in person. She had two half sisters who seemed to hate each other in equal measure to their ambivalence toward her. Just when she thought life couldn't get worse, it did.

"We can talk in more detail about the assets and debts Niall left behind when you've had time to process everything," the attorney said, the words a clear dismissal.

She tucked a strand of hair behind her ear. "I thought I'd be here for a day at the most."

He chuckled. "Niall didn't make things easy—not when he was alive and not now. It will take a while to even begin to sort this out. Welcome to Magnolia."

Don't miss
The Magnolia Sisters *by Michelle Major,*
available April 2020 wherever
HQN books and ebooks are sold.

HQNBooks.com